Tammy tucked a strand of hair behind her ear. "Is something wrong, Doc?"

"Wrong? No." Hell no. It's just that he... Damn. "I didn't recognize you at first, and it kind of... threw me for a loop, I guess."

"It's the dress."

No, it was more than the dress—although the style and fabric certainly spotlighted the woman he'd failed to see before.

He probably ought to say something else, to comment about the new Tammy. But Mike was...dumbstruck. Awestruck. Maybe even a bit moonstruck.

Damn. He couldn't seem to take his eyes off little Tammy Byrd, who didn't seem so little anymore— in spite of her short stature. She couldn't be much taller than five foot one. Still Mother Nature had packed a whole lot of woman in her.

He couldn't seem to do anything but gawk at her and stumble along in his thoughts. Of course, it was just the metamorphosis that had him amazed.

Wasn't it?

Dear Reader,

Ever since my first Harlequin Special Edition title hit the shelves in 2002, I dreamed of creating a series with my best friends and critique partners, Crystal Green and Sheri WhiteFeather. Crystal and Sheri had the same dream, and after a weekend retreat spent at Crystal's house, we came up the idea for Byrds of a Feather.

We set the stories on a cattle ranch in Buckshot Hills, Texas. Then we threw in a family feud, as well as an antique feather bed. According to family legend, the dreams had while sleeping in the antique bed are said to come true. Add a little romance to that intriguing mix, and you have all the makings for a great read.

I am so glad you chose *Tammy and the Doctor,* the first book in the series. As you turn the pages, you'll meet Tammy Byrd, who was raised on a ranch by her single dad and two rough and tough older brothers.

When Tammy and her family are called to her dying grandfather's bedside, she meets Dr. Mike Sanchez, who turns the cowgirl's heart every which way but loose. And while "Doc" hardly notices Tammy at first, she sets out to shake her tomboy image and become the woman of his dreams.

Happy reading!

Judy

TAMMY AND THE DOCTOR

JUDY DUARTE

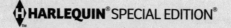

HARLEQUIN® SPECIAL EDITION®

Recycling programs
for this product may
not exist in your area.

ISBN-13: 978-0-373-65731-5

TAMMY AND THE DOCTOR

Copyright © 2013 by Judy Duarte

Printed in U.S.A.

Books by Judy Duarte

JUDY DUARTE

always knew there was a book inside her, but since English was her least favorite subject in school, she never considered herself a writer. An avid reader who enjoys a happy ending, Judy couldn't shake the dream of creating a book of her own.

Her dream became a reality in March 2002, when Silhouette Special Edition released her first book, *Cowboy Courage*. Since then she has published more than twenty novels. Her stories have touched the hearts of readers around the world. And in July 2005 Judy won a prestigious Readers' Choice Award for *The Rich Man's Son*.

Judy makes her home near the beach in Southern California. When she's not cooped up in her writing cave, she's spending time with her somewhat enormous but delightfully close family.

To the best friends and critique partners ever:
Crystal Green and Sheri WhiteFeather.
Where would I be without you?

Chapter One

There were a lot of things Tammy Byrd would rather be doing on a Saturday afternoon than driving five hours to meet a bunch of relatives she'd never met, but there was no way around it.

Her paternal grandfather was dying, and he'd called his estranged family home.

She supposed she ought to feel something after hearing of the poor man's plight, like sadness, grief or compassion, but any kind of relationship with him had been lost to her, thanks to a falling-out he'd had with her father years ago.

Apparently, now that Jasper J. "Tex" Byrd was about to face his maker, he was going to try and make things right. At least, that's how Tammy had it figured.

When she'd first heard of the old man's request, she'd assumed her stubborn, my-way-or-the-highway daddy would have dug in his boot heels and refused to go.

She'd also wondered what her dad would say when he learned that she was going to make the trek on her own.

But he'd blown her away by announcing he was going to make the trip and insisting that she and her brothers join him.

Whatever his reason, be it guilt, love or a need to set things to right, her father, who never took orders from anyone, had caved to the old man's request.

Tammy's brothers had been summoned, too, but they were fishing in a remote area of Montana and couldn't be easily reached for at least several days, maybe a week. Still, she knew they'd be on the first flight they could find back to Texas. Family had always been important to them. Well, at least, their immediate family was.

Her father would be coming later, too. She supposed she could have waited until after he'd had his appointment for his annual physical and rode with him, but she'd wanted to have her own vehicle handy. Besides, she was intrigued by the whole idea of family feuds and secrets. So she'd packed her bag this morning, prepared to meet the rest of her family—a dying grandfather, an uncle and two cousins she'd never met. Then she'd slid behind the wheel of her little pickup and left her daddy's ranch.

Five hours later, with the satellite radio tuned to a classic country-western station, an empty diet soda can in her cup holder and the printout of the directions on the seat beside her, she neared her final destination in Buckshot Hills.

She slowed as she reached a cluster of oak trees,

which her father had told her to watch for, then searched for the sign that indicated she'd reached Flying B Road.

There it was, a bold wrought-iron-and-metallic creation that was as big as day—and as ornate as all getout.

Before she could turn off one road and onto the other, a black Dodge Ram pickup with mud flaps roared around her. As it passed, the left rear tire hit a mud puddle and shot a big splash of dirty water at her little white truck.

The jerk.

She was about to lay on the horn, but held back. After all, it might be one of the relatives, and there was no need to get off on a bad foot before they'd had a chance to meet face-to-face.

Realizing she'd have to wash the truck to get the bug spatters off the windshield, anyway, she shrugged off her annoyance and turned right onto the road that led to the ranch house.

As she drove, she scanned the rolling hills and the lush pastures dotted with grazing cattle. It was a beautiful piece of property, and she wondered what it would have been like growing up on a place like this, instead of back in Grass Valley, on the much smaller spread her daddy had inherited from her maternal grandfather.

When she neared the big, sprawling house, with a wraparound porch, she looked for a place to park her truck. Then she chose a spot next to the Dodge Ram.

A dark-haired man who appeared to be in his early thirties still sat in the driver's seat, talking on his cell phone.

He was too young to be her uncle. Was he one of the cousins?

She pulled in beside him and shut off her ignition, just as he opened the driver's door and climbed from the cab.

Unlike the cowboys or ranch hands she'd grown up with, he wore a pair of polished loafers, black slacks and a light blue button-down shirt. A thick head of dark hair and an olive complexion boasted of a Hispanic bloodline.

Tammy blew out a little whistle. She didn't find many men worth a second glance. She was too busy competing with the ones she rubbed elbows with each day. But this one was…different.

And she couldn't help sitting in her seat, her hands braced on the steering wheel, her heart pounding to beat the band.

Who was he?

She had no idea, but she hoped he wasn't a blood relative.

He pulled a worn leather satchel from the cab of his truck, the kind an old-fashioned doctor who made house calls might carry.

But there wasn't anything old-fashioned about *him*.

When he looked her way and caught her eye, he gave a little smile and a nod of acknowledgment. Then he made his way toward the house.

For the life of her, all she could do was sit and watch him go.

By the time she'd cleared her head of goofy, hormonal thoughts and gathered her courage for an introduction of some kind, he was climbing up the steps to the house. So she quickly got out of the truck and grabbed her suitcase from the bed. Then she followed him up the steps to the front door.

As she neared the porch, a woman with silver-streaked black hair swung open the door as if she'd been waiting for the man all day and had just heard him drive up.

"Good afternoon," she said. "Come on in, Doc."

So he was the doctor—her grandfather's personal physician, no doubt. The fact that a man like him was willing to make house calls was enough to make a girl feel faint—or to claim feeling that way just so she could get his attention and spend some time alone with him.

"Thanks," Doc said. "How's Tex doing today, Tina?"

"Not as good as he was yesterday, but maybe that's because he didn't sleep too well last night."

"Can I get you anything?" the woman—Tina—asked as she stepped aside to let the doctor into the house. "Coffee maybe? Barbara just whipped up a batch of blueberry muffins."

"Sounds great. I'd never turn down anything Barbara baked. She's got to be the best cook in the county."

As Doc stepped into the house, the woman at the door noticed Tammy standing just a few feet away, her suitcase in hand. She hoped she wasn't caught gaping like a lovesick puppy.

So she rallied, reclaiming her runaway thoughts.

"Good afternoon," Tammy said, realizing she'd better introduce herself. "I'm William's daughter. Mr. Byrd is expecting me."

The older woman greeted her with a slow smile and an outstretched hand. "I'm Tina Crandall, your grandfather's housekeeper. Please come in. We've been expecting you."

Tammy carried her suitcase inside.

"I'm afraid he's not able to talk with you at the moment," Tina said. "As you can see, the doctor just arrived. But in the meantime, I can show you to your room so you can freshen up."

Tammy glanced down at the blue plaid flannel shirt she wore, as well as the denim jeans. She'd showered this morning, and her clothes were clean. As far as she was concerned, she'd dressed for the occasion.

Another woman might have wanted to powder her nose or apply some lipstick, but Tammy never had cottoned to using makeup. But she wouldn't mind checking out the room where she'd be staying during the unexpected homecoming. "Sure, that'd be great. Thanks."

Tina led Tammy across the scarred wood plank flooring in the entry and into a large, rugged living room, with white plastered walls, dark beams and an amazing stone fireplace adorned with an antlered deer head.

So this is where her daddy had grown up and learned to be a man. It certainly had a masculine decor.

In a way, the style appealed to Tammy. As the only girl in a family of men, she'd grown up trying to not only keep up with her brothers, but also outdo them. In fact, she'd become so competent as a ranch hand on her daddy's ranch, that not many of the cowboys could best her.

"As soon as you freshen up," Tina said, glancing over her shoulder, "I'll take you into the kitchen, where we'll get you fed. Barbara has been cooking and baking for the past two days, just getting ready for y'all."

"Sounds good to me." Tammy wondered how wealthy "Tex," or rather her grandfather, was if he could afford to hire one woman to clean his house and another to fix his meals.

Back home, Tammy handled all the household chores, especially the cooking. And she wasn't half-bad at it, either.

'Course she complained about the chore every chance she got. It wouldn't do her a lick of good to let the men she lived with know that she actually liked puttering around the kitchen.

"Am I the first to arrive?" Tammy asked.

"So far. But I expect the others will be rolling in soon."

Tammy brushed her free hand along the sides of denim jeans, glad she'd gotten here first since her nerves were so jumpy. She wasn't looking forward to meeting the people who were strangers to her. Still, at the same time, she looked forward to it. It ought to be…interesting.

But not nearly as interesting as having a chance to see the handsome doctor again.

Doc didn't seem to notice that Tammy was alive, which, surprisingly, was more than a little disappointing.

For the first time in her life, she wished that she'd packed more than jeans and Western shirts to wear. But she couldn't have done that when she didn't wear—or even *own*—anything else. Why waste her money or her closet space on stuff she wouldn't have any use for on a working cattle ranch?

But maybe she should have considered something a little more…feminine, at least for times like this.

Oh, for Pete's sake. She'd never been the least bit feminine, and had never regretted that fact.

Okay, so she'd regretted it once. In high school, she'd taken a liking to Bobby Hankin, who'd sat across from her in biology. He'd been nicer to her than most of the other guys, so she'd flirted with him—or at least, tried to. And it had backfired on her. She'd overheard him talking about it to a friend, saying that Tam-boy had taken a fancy to him. So from then on she'd set aside any girly or romantic thoughts.

She'd best remember that now. After all, she really ought to be more concerned about her reasons for being at the Flying B in the first place. Somewhere down the hall, Jasper J. "Tex" Byrd lay dying, and Tammy owed him her condolences, to say the least.

Ever since learning that the family had been called home to Buckshot Hills, she'd been champing at the bit to meet her grandfather for the very first time. And while she was certainly looking forward to doing that, she was also dead-set on introducing herself. It wouldn't be so hard to think about her first introduction to Tex, if she wasn't so focused on meeting the doctor who'd just stopped by to examine him.

Mike Sanchez removed the stethoscope from Tex Byrd's chest, then took a seat in the chair beside the bed. "How are those pain meds I prescribed working for you?"

"They're taking the edge off, I suppose."

Mike could increase the dosage. He could also prescribe morphine, although he'd been holding off on that until closer to the end. Maybe it was time to consider it now. Tex would be having a lot of pain in upcoming days, and he was going to need all the help medical science could give him to deal with it.

The white-haired old rancher shifted his weight in the bed, as if trying to find a more comfortable spot. Then he grimaced, suggesting the move hadn't helped much.

As he settled back on the pillows propping him up, he said, "My boys and grandchildren agreed to come home. Did I tell you that, Doc?"

"You'd mentioned extending the invitation to them."

Tex closed his eyes for a moment, then opened them again. "I wasn't sure what they'd tell me. That blasted feud had gone on for so damn long, I figured they might not give a rip about me or the Flying B."

"For what it's worth," Mike said, "I think one of them just arrived."

A smile stretched across the old man's craggy face, softening the age lines and providing a hint of color to his wan complexion. "Oh, yeah? Who'd you see?"

"I'm not sure. A girl—or rather a woman, I guess. She's probably about twenty, with long, dark hair pulled back in a ponytail of some kind. She was driving a little white pickup."

"Was she all dolled up like a city girl? Or wearing pants like a tomboy?"

"She wasn't wearing any makeup at all. And she had on a pair of worn denim jeans and a blue flannel shirt."

"Then that must be Tammy," Tex said, his tired gray eyes lighting up. "She's William's girl. And quite the cowboy, I hear. She can outride, outrope and outspit the best of 'em."

Mike wouldn't know about that. The girl certainly appeared to be a tomboy, but she was also petite. He wasn't sure if she could hold her own or not.

"I thought you told me that you'd never met your grandchildren," Mike said.

The old man gave a single shrug. "I've seen pictures of them. But only because I hired a private investigator a few years back. And now…" He lifted an aged, work-roughened, liver-spotted hand and plopped it down on the mattress. "I'm glad that I did. It would have been tough finding them all with only a short time to do it."

Tex only had a few weeks left to live, although it was always hard to guess just how long for sure. The rancher was a tough old bird. And he might just will himself to stay alive long enough to put his family back together again.

From what Mike had heard, there'd been some huge family blowup over thirty years ago. Both of Tex's boys had taken off in anger, leaving the Flying B and Buckshot Hills far behind. But no one seemed to know any more details than that. And Doc didn't plan to stick around any longer than he had to, so none of it really mattered to him.

Tex took a deep, weary breath, then slowly let it out. He'd be needing oxygen soon, so Mike would place the order so it would be on hand.

"You know," the old man said, "I wasn't happy about switching doctors. I'd hoped Doc Reynolds would be back in Buckshot Hills by now. But you seem to know your stuff—at least, for a young fellow fresh out of medical school."

Mike never planned to fill in for the local doctor who was being treated for a brain tumor in Boston. But then again, Mike had a debt to repay. And spending six to nine months in Podunk, Texas, appeared to be the only way he could do that.

Practicing medicine—or rather, "doctoring folks"—was a heck of a lot different in a small town than it was in the city, but he was learning the ropes and doing the best he could do without the high-tech labs and specialty hospitals nearby. And after nearly four months in Buckshot Hills, he was counting down the days until he could return to Philadelphia.

Mike had grown up there, and his mom still worked as a housekeeper for George Ballard, a very wealthy businessman, a widower who'd never had children. George had taken a liking to Mike's mom. Not in a romantic sense, but he'd come to respect her work ethic, her integrity and her loyalty. And that had led to yearly bonuses and unexpected paid vacations.

When George had learned that Mike had been accepted to medical school, he'd offered to foot the bill.

It had been a generous offer, an amazing one. And Mike had vowed to pay him back. But George wouldn't consider it. Instead, he'd said, "If I ever have need of a personal physician, I'll expect you to drop everything and come to my aid."

Of course, Mike had readily agreed, although he hadn't realized how serious the guy had been about the terms of the debt. Or that his benefactor would eventually become romantically involved with a woman whose beloved uncle, Stanley Reynolds, was an ailing country doctor in Texas.

Without the new treatment for a brain tumor that was only available at a specialized clinic on the east coast, Dr. Reynolds would die. But he'd refused to leave his patients in Buckshot Hills without medical care for the extended period of time his treatment was expected to take.

So George had called in the favor, asking Mike to spend the first six months after his residency covering for Dr. Reynolds.

While disappointed at the assignment—after all, Buckshot Hills was a far cry from the city life he loved or the plans and dreams he'd made—Mike had agreed. He just hoped that, when his debt had been paid, the offer he'd received from a top-notch medical group in Philadelphia would still be available to him.

But he supposed he shouldn't complain. A lot of doctors were strapped with huge student loans, and he wasn't.

"Thanks for stopping by," Tex said. "Will I see you tomorrow?"

"Yes, but not until late afternoon or early evening." Mike reached out a hand to his patient, leaving him with a parting shake. "Call me if you need anything between now and then."

"Will do. Thanks, Doc."

As Mike left Tex, he headed down the hall past several bedrooms that had been prepared for the Byrd homecoming. As he made his way to the living room, he spotted Tex's granddaughter seated on the leather sofa. He'd pretty much passed over her earlier, so he decided to make an effort to be more polite before he left.

"Tammy?" he asked.

Her lips parted, and her eyes, the color of the summer sky, widened. "Yes?"

He reached out a hand to greet her. "We weren't introduced earlier. But I'm Dr. Mike Sanchez, your grandfather's physician."

She stood, brushed her hand against her denim-clad hip then gave him a customary shake. Her grip held a surprising strength for a petite woman. "It's nice to meet you, Doc."

Tex had called her a tomboy, and he'd had that right, although cowgirl seemed more like it. Either way, she certainly didn't put much stock in lotions, makeup or perfume. He caught the clean scent of bar soap and shampoo, but the fragrance was more generic than anything.

"How's he doing?" she asked.

"About the same as yesterday. He tires easily. And he's uncomfortable at times."

She nodded, as if trying to take it all in, to make sense of the cancer that had consumed his once strong body.

According to what Tex had told Mike, he'd never met his grandchildren. So he wondered how they'd taken the news of his terminal illness. Did they grieve for what they could have had, if the family hadn't been prone to holding grudges?

Or were they more interested in an inheritance?

He supposed it didn't matter. It really wasn't any of

his business. He was just here to make sure Tex was as comfortable as he could be.

"It was nice of you to drive out here to see him," Tammy said. "Our doctor back in Weldon makes us come to his office in town. In fact, most of us learned how to do a lot of the doctoring ourselves, just so we didn't have to drive twenty miles."

Mike hadn't planned to make house calls, as was the custom of the doctor before him. But he made an exception for a couple of patients, including Tex Byrd, who'd refused to be hospitalized in Granite Falls, a larger town about thirty miles away.

"Your grandfather is a stubborn man," Mike said. "He wouldn't have any medical care at all if I didn't make the trip out here."

Mike had also promised Stanley Reynolds that he'd look over his patients as if they were Mike's own family members—an agreement he'd made as part of the debt repayment plan.

So here he was.

Tammy bit down on her bottom lip. "Can I ask you something?"

"Sure."

"What's he like?" Her eyes were an almost dazzling shade of blue. And the way she was looking at him right now, as if he held all the answers she'd ever need, was a little humbling.

Mike reminded himself that she'd never met the man and that her curiosity was to be expected. So he told her what he knew—or what he'd heard. "He's a hard worker. And as honest as the day is long. He's a bit testy, though. Rumor has it he's been that way for years."

Tex, who was in his late seventies, was actually one of the most ornery, cantankerous old men Mike had ever met. But he was also a real hoot at times, and Mike couldn't help admiring him for a lot of reasons—his work ethic, his gumption and his desperate efforts to bring his family home before his death.

"He's a good man," Mike added. "One you can be proud of. He's also well-respected in the community."

"Thanks. I'm…" She bit down on her bottom lip again, then looked up at him with those amazing eyes. "Well, I guess you could say I'm a bit nervous."

"That's understandable."

She straightened, drawing herself up to her full height, which couldn't be much more than five feet. "I don't usually admit stuff like that, but you being a doctor and all…" Her cheeks flushed a rosy shade of pink, which was at odds with the masculine clothing she wore and her tough-guy stance.

"Your secret's safe with me," Mike said. Then he gave her a little wink and placed his hand on her shoulder. "It's probably only fair to tell you that I think your grandpa is a little nervous about meeting you, too."

She smiled and blinked—once, twice, a third time.

If Mike didn't know better, he'd think she was giving him one of those flirty southern-belle eye flutters. But it couldn't be that. Maybe she was blinking back tears.

She might have even gotten a speck of dust or something in her eye.

"Are you okay?" he asked.

"I…uh…" She swiped her hand across one eye, rubbing it. "I'm fine. It was just a stray lash. That's all."

At that moment, Tina returned to the living room

carrying a mug and a blueberry muffin balanced on a small plate. "You're not leaving, are you, Doc?"

"I have to get back to the office. I also have a couple more patients to see on the way, too."

Tina handed the cup and plate to him. "Then why don't you take this with you?"

"Thanks." He took the coffee and muffin. "I'll bring back the dishes when I return."

"Are you coming back tomorrow?" the housekeeper asked.

"Yes, but probably not until the dinner hour. I hope that'll be all right."

"No problem whatsoever," Tina said. "We're just glad that you're willing to drive out here to see Tex. I'll let Barbara know to set an extra plate at the table."

Mike thanked her, then turned to Tammy. "It was nice meeting you."

"Same here." Her gaze snared his, as if she'd set her sights on him and wasn't about to let go.

He could be wrong about that, though. And he certainly hoped that he was. All he needed was for his patient's granddaughter to start crushing on him.

Little Tammy Byrd might have the prettiest blue eyes he'd ever seen, but Mike wasn't interested in romance—especially in a place like Buckshot Hills. And even if by some strange twist of Fate he got involved with one of the local women, it sure as hell wouldn't be a cowgirl.

Chapter Two

As Dr. Sanchez left the house, Tammy watched him go.

Darn it! Clearly, her attempts at flirting had failed yet again. What was she doing wrong?

"Can I get you something to drink, Miss Byrd? Coffee's fresh. We also have some lemonade or ice tea."

Tammy turned to Tina, the housekeeper, who'd shown her to the guestroom in which she'd be staying and must have been waiting for her to settle in and then return to the main part of the house.

"Lemonade sounds great," Tammy said. "Thank you."

The woman nodded, then left Tammy alone in the spacious living room.

So now what? Should she sit down on the leather sofa again? Or would she be out of line if she wandered around the room, checking out the furnishings and trying to get a handle on the old man who called the Flying B home?

As Tina's footsteps faded into silence, Tammy crossed the room to the bay window and peered outside, beyond the porch, to see if anyone else had arrived while she'd been putting away her things in the bedroom she'd been assigned.

The Dodge Ram was gone, of course, which was too bad. She would have liked spending some time with Doc and getting to know him a little better.

She'd expected to meet a bunch of new family members, each one bringing a unique personality and mindset to the mix. But she hadn't been prepared to run in to the handsome doctor making a house call.

Boy howdy, was Doc Sanchez a sight for sore eyes.

When he'd finally introduced himself, a rush of hormones had slammed into her, taking her breath away. She'd never felt anything like it. Even if she let her thoughts roll all the way back to grade school, when the kids teased her and called her Tam-boy, she couldn't come up with a single fellow who'd set her heart on end.

Yet in one brief moment, Mike Sanchez, also known as Doc, had swept her off her booted little feet.

At least, that's what it felt like to a woman inexperienced in that sort of thing. And to be honest, it left her a little unbalanced.

Tammy didn't get flustered too easily, since she usually kept to herself and didn't pay any mind to mingling, or cultivating new relationships—male or female. And there was a good reason for it, too. Women didn't seem to find her worth talking to, and men never took her seriously until she showed them her mettle.

But meeting Doc had her reevaluating a few things she'd once thought were carved in stone. It also had her doing things she'd never expected to do—like trying to let him know that she was sweet on him, although it hadn't worked out too well.

Why in Sam Hill had she tried to flutter her lashes at him?

Talk about awkward and out-of-step.

When Doc had asked if she was okay, her cheeks had burned as hot as the asphalt at high noon in mid-August, and she hadn't known quite what to say or how to recover her pride.

After that disappointing experience in high school, she'd quit trying to get a guy's attention—well, not unless she was trying to outdo him at something. And meeting Doc, feeling that rush of hormones, hadn't been one of those times.

When it was all said and done, she doubted she could best him at anything. Or if she'd even want to.

"Here you go," Tina said, offering Tammy a glass of lemonade and a napkin to go with it.

"Thank you."

"I know you're probably interested in meeting your grandfather, but he just had his medication. I checked on him a few moments ago, and he's asleep."

"That's okay. I can wait."

Tina clasped her hands in front of her. "Is there anything I can get you? Anything you need?"

"No, ma'am. I'm good."

Tina nodded, then turned and walked away—heading to the kitchen, Tammy guessed. And that was fine with her. She didn't like making small talk with people she didn't know. So she used the time to study the brightly colored southwestern artwork hanging on the walls and to check out the various sculptures and knickknacks that adorned the built-in bookshelf to the right of the hearth.

All the while, she sipped her lemonade, drinking it down. Boy, did that hit the spot.

When she'd finished it, she glanced at the empty glass, wondering what she ought to do with it. Maybe she should return it to the kitchen. So she crossed the living room, heading in the same direction Tina had gone.

As she neared a doorway, the sound of whispers caused her to pause. She listened, overhearing the housekeeper say something about the "family rift."

Unable to help herself, she stepped aside and leaned against the wall, next to the doorjamb.

"To tell you the truth," Tina said, her voice low, "I'd given up thinking either of those boys would ever return to the Flying B."

"I know what you mean," the other woman said. "After nearly thirty-five years, there's been too much water under the bridge."

"You're probably right. I'll never forget the day it happened. The awful words they said to each other. The anger…" Tina clicked her tongue.

Tammy stood still, not daring to go closer, not wanting to stop the conversation from unfolding.

"Poor Tex," the other woman said. "All the family he had left in the world was those two boys. And to think that they would both run off and leave him like that."

But *why?* Tammy wondered. Her father had never said, other than to imply there was bad blood between them.

"At least they both came back before it was too late," Tina added.

"They haven't returned *yet*. And after being so stubborn for so long, I suppose anything could happen."

Tammy's father had told her he would arrive at the ranch late this afternoon. He wouldn't back out now, would he?

She leaned closer to the open doorway, trying her best to hear more, to learn more.

Her father and her uncle had been at odds with each other and with Grandpa Byrd, too, which was why she'd never met her other family members. But she'd never heard any of the details. In fact, up until today, she'd never cared enough to ask.

But now her curiosity was mounting with each beat of her heart.

What had caused the rift? And why had it lasted so long?

She waited for several minutes, but the voices stilled, as if the conversation had just vaporized.

When it became clear that neither the housekeeper nor the cook would bring up the subject of the family feud again, Tammy stepped away from the wall she'd been leaning against and entered the bright and sunny kitchen with her empty glass in hand.

"The lemonade was great," she said, addressing the housekeeper while scanning the spacious room with its old-style gingham curtains and modern appliances. "Where should I put this?"

"I'm sorry, Miss Byrd." Tina got up from her seat at a polished, dark oak table. "I should have picked up that glass for you."

"I don't mind picking up after myself. And please call me Tammy." She offered a smile, hoping that striking up a friendship of sorts with the household help would provide her with the details she wanted to know.

"All right. Then Tammy it is." Tina took the glass from her and turned to a short, heavyset woman who was peeling potatoes at the sink. "Barbara, this is William's youngest."

The matronly cook, her hair tinted a coppery shade of red, her cheeks rosy and plump, reached for a paper towel. After drying her pudgy hands, she reached out to Tammy. "It's nice to meet you, honey. Is your daddy coming?"

"He sure is." Tammy accepted the handshake, hoping she was telling the truth and that her father would follow through as planned. "In fact, he should be here before dark."

Both women glanced at each other, their gazes making a quick and intimate connection, before turning their focus back on Tammy and offering nods and smiles.

"That's good news," Tina said. "I haven't seen your daddy since he left for college."

What? No mention of the family argument? The angry words thrown at each other? The night it— whatever *it* was—had happened?

Hadn't the women said both boys had run off, leaving Tex alone for almost thirty-five years?

If Tammy had known either of the women a little

better, she would have quizzed them further. As it was, she'd let it go—at least, for now.

But come hell or high water, she was going to get to the bottom of it. And she would start by cornering her father as soon as he arrived.

Sure enough, William Travis Byrd arrived at the Flying B just as the sun was setting.

Tammy, who'd been gazing out the big bay window in the living room, was on her feet and out the door before he could turn off the ignition of the restored 1975 Pontiac Trans Am he'd owned for as long as any of his three kids could remember.

The classic vehicle only had 27,000 miles on it and looked as though it had just rolled off the assembly line, with its original camel-tan cloth interior and spiffy gold paint, including the firebird on the hood. Needless to say, the V-8 sports car was William Byrd's pride and joy, so Tammy was more than a little surprised to see that he'd driven it all this distance, when he usually kept it in a garage back at the family ranch in Grass Valley.

Had he left the Flying B in that same car on that fateful day? If so, had he decided to return the same way—just as angry, just as stubborn, just as determined to hold a grudge?

"Hey," she said, as she stepped off the porch. "How was the drive?"

Her dad shut the driver's door. "Not bad. How was yours?"

"It was good—easy and quiet."

Her dad nodded at the house. "What's going on in there?"

"Not much. I haven't met Tex—or rather my grandfather—yet. Right before I got here, he took some pain medication, so they tell me he's sleeping."

Her dad, his once blond hair faded to gray, tensed. Did it bother him to know that Tex was hurting...and badly? That he truly was dying?

Tammy couldn't imagine why it wouldn't. Why else would he have come back to the Flying B?

Once she crossed the yard and reached his side, she broached the question that had been burning inside her ever since she'd arrived. "I have something I've been meaning to ask you."

"What's that?"

She folded her arms over her chest and shifted her weight to one leg. "What caused that falling-out you had with your dad and brother?"

His lips tightened, and his brow furrowed. Yet he didn't respond.

About the time she figured he wouldn't, he said, "My brother did something unforgivable. And my father was in cahoots."

"What did he do?"

For a moment, her father's stance eased and his expression softened. He lifted his hand and cupped her cheek, his eyes glistening. Then he stiffened again, rolling back the gentle side of himself that he rarely showed anyone. "That was a long time ago, Tam."

Yes, it was. But he'd held on to his anger—or someone else had—for *thirty-five years*. So pretending to brush it all off wasn't working. And nothing he said, short of spilling the beans, was going to convince her that it hadn't been a big deal. It must have been huge.

"You know," her father said, removing his hand from her cheek and scanning the yard, "now that I'm here, I'm going to take a little walk before it gets dark."

"What are you planning to do?"

He shrugged. "I'm just going to check things out, see what's changed and what hasn't. I might even look for the foreman and ask him if any of the old ranch hands are still around. Some of them were friends of mine."

"Okay. But, Daddy, what—"

He raised his hand like a traffic cop, halting her words with a warning look. "If things had been different, Tammy, I never would have met your mother or had you and your brothers. So just drop it."

Then he walked away, letting her know the discussion was over.

Trouble was, everyone in the immediate family knew Tammy had a curious streak a mile wide. And now that she knew there was some kind of dark secret to uncover, she'd be darned if she'd back down and let it go.

Moments later, as her father reached the barn and Tammy was still standing in the drive, a woman drove up in a bright red convertible.

Tammy watched as she parked, then climbed from the car and removed a stylish, autumn-colored scarf from her head, revealing straight, shoulder-length blond hair.

She wore a pair of boots and a brown skirt that had to be fashionable as well as expensive. Yet more remarkable was a cream-colored sweater that showed off an amazing set of bazooms.

Would you look at that? Tammy had a pair a lot like 'em, but she kept hers hidden behind loose-fitting shirts, like the blue flannel one she had on today. After all, the darn things usually got in the way when she worked.

Besides, she'd never liked getting *that* kind of attention from men.

But then again, after meeting Doc today... Well, she wasn't so sure about anything anymore.

Either way, she removed her hands from the front pockets of her jeans and moseyed a bit closer to the much taller woman, introducing herself and her connection to Tex.

The blonde stuck out a soft, manicured hand and gave her a solid greeting. "I'm Donna, Sam's daughter."

"Nice to meet you." Tammy tried out a friendly smile on her attractive cousin and was glad to see it returned.

Well, it wasn't one of those full-on, warm-and-fuzzy smiles that said, "Let's be friends." Hers was more like, "If I have to be here, I may as well make the best of it."

But Tammy could live with that.

"Have my father or my sister, Jenna, arrived yet?" Donna asked.

"Nope, not yet. So far, it's just you, me and my dad. My two brothers, Aidan and Nathan, won't get here until later this week. They're on a fishing trip out in the wilds of Montana, and we have no way of even contacting them until later this week."

Donna nodded, as if she understood, yet something in her gut told Tammy the stylish, citified woman had never gone fishing or hunting or camping before. Heck, she didn't even look as though she could handle a temporary visit on a ranch.

Of course, the conclusion Tammy came to when

she took in her stylishly cut hair, the carefully applied makeup and that womanly shape.

"I suppose I should go inside and let someone know I'm here," Donna said, as she reached into the backseat of the convertible and took out a suitcase. Then she pressed a button that caused the top to roll down.

"The housekeeper's name is Tina," Tammy said. "She'll probably show you to your room. There certainly seems to be a lot of them, which means we won't have to double up."

Meeting her new cousins was one thing. But sharing their sleeping quarters was another.

Tammy scanned the sprawling house, which had to be three times the size of the one she shared with her father in Grass Valley. And their home was nearly two thousand square feet.

As Donna strode toward the wraparound porch, her hips swayed in a way that looked natural and not at all fake. And Tammy couldn't help being a bit envious.

She wondered how old her cousin Donna was—certainly more than Tammy's twenty-five years. Was she thirty yet? It was hard to say. Women who wore makeup could hide a lot of the telltale signs of aging.

As if on its own accord, her hand lifted to her own face, which she never bothered to cover with color or protect with sunblock. Then she scoffed at the brief moment of insecurity and shoved her hands back in her pockets.

Rather than follow Donna back into the house, she scanned the yard, taking in the big barn, the corrals and the outbuildings.

About the time she decided that it might be fun to

take off on her own little exploration of the Flying B, another engine sounded in the distance. She waited and watched as a blue pickup arrived.

Another blonde sat behind the wheel. She really didn't resemble Donna all that much, but Tammy figured it had to be Jenna—especially when she climbed out of the truck and reached for a suitcase in back. Who else could it be?

Tammy gave her a once-over, noting that she was wearing jeans. But hers weren't as worn or baggy as Tammy's. In fact, they looked brand-spanking-new.

Her frilly white cotton blouse didn't hug her curves, like Donna's sweater had. And unlike Donna, with her womanly curves, Jenna was slight and willowy. But she was just as pretty, just as feminine.

And to be honest, it was enough to make Tammy want to squirm right out of her worn denim jeans.

She sure hoped her cousins didn't set their sights on Doc, because if either of them did, Tammy would be left in the dust.

How in blazes was she supposed to compete with two beautiful women?

For the first time in her life, Tammy—who could hold her own on a ranch full of men—felt sorely lacking.

Tammy's father had yet to return after his walk, but that didn't stop Tina from entering the living room, where Jenna and Donna had just joined Tammy, and suggesting they come to the kitchen and eat the pot roast Barbara had prepared.

"Since everyone will be arriving at different times,"

the older woman added, "I don't see any point in making the rest of you wait to eat."

The young women, who'd barely had a chance to strike up a conversation, looked at each other, then agreed and followed Tina to the kitchen, where Barbara had set the table for three.

"Later on," Tina added, "I'll take you to meet Tex. I know he plans to have a family powwow after everyone gets here, but that's probably not going to take place until next weekend. In the meantime when he's awake, I'm sure he'd like a chance to talk to each of you."

If Tammy were the dying man, she'd want to meet with each person individually, too. And she'd start off by calling in the sons who'd left the ranch and created lives and families of their own. But then again, most people didn't do things the way Tammy did. Besides, it was Tex Byrd's call.

Once Barbara had served them, the two older women left them to eat in silence.

After several uncomfortable minutes, Tammy set down her fork and leaned forward in her seat. "Okay, you guys. I think this whole family-reunion thing is weird, not to mention as awkward as all get-out."

Donna looked up from her plate, her eyebrows arched. "I was just thinking the same thing."

Jenna nodded her agreement.

So they were all feeling the same thing—and probably just as curious about what had created all the ill feelings.

"Do either of you know anything about that falling-out?" Tammy asked.

"I'm afraid not, but I've always been curious." Jenna

glanced at her sister, then back to Tammy. "I knew we had an uncle and a grandfather, but that's about it. My dad never talked about his childhood or life on the Flying B."

"Neither did mine," Tammy said. "I asked about it a couple of times, but he refused to answer." Tammy decided not to mention the talk she'd had with her dad just a few hours ago—or the revelation that Jenna and Donna's father had done something "unforgivable."

"Maybe we'll hear more about it at that family 'pow-wow' we're supposed to have," Jenna said.

Tammy didn't know about that. "After thirty-five years of silence, it's hard to imagine any of those involved opening up."

"That's too bad." Jenna lifted her napkin and blotted her lips. "Having an unsolved family problem can affect other relationships down the road."

She was probably right, although it hadn't seemed to affect Tammy's father or his one and only relationship. Her parents had been happily married—at least, that's what she'd heard.

"Our parents divorced when we were young," Donna said. "And our dad never remarried."

"We lived with our mother until we were eight and ten," Jenna added. "And when Mom died, we moved in with our dad. By that time, I just assumed that we'd never be close with the Byrd side of the family. But that doesn't mean I didn't want to."

Until Tex Byrd had called the family home, Tammy hadn't given that side of her family a whole lot of thought. And even now, she wasn't so sure she'd like her relatives, although Jenna and Donna seemed okay.

Donna didn't appear to be as forthright as her sister. In fact, the two didn't seem to be especially close. But what did Tammy know about them—or about having relationships with other women?

When it came right down to it, she didn't have a single thing in common with either of her cousins—other than some shared DNA.

Well, that and the fact they'd lost their mother, too.

"I never knew my mama," Tammy admitted. "She died when I was two, so my dad raised me on his own."

"I'm sorry to hear you lost your mother so young," Jenna said. "A father doesn't always understand what it's like to be a girl growing up to be a woman."

That's for sure. Tammy smiled. "I guess that's why it was easier not to even try to be a lady."

Oh, no. Had she really said *that*? Out loud?

"I mean," Tammy said in an attempt to explain herself, "who needs high heels and prom dresses, anyway?"

She'd never really missed the goofy adolescent glamour. Well, not until this very moment in time, when she realized that neither Jenna nor Donna would have a lick of trouble getting Doc's attention when he showed up at the ranch tomorrow.

And now look at her—trying to reach out and befriend two women who'd probably always be strangers to her. But something told her that Doc wouldn't give a flying leap about how good she was with a lasso, so she was going to have to learn the ropes of being a woman.

And she knew just the women who could offer her some helpful feminine hints, if they were willing. After all, they were older and wiser when it came to that sort of thing.

But could she lay her heart and soul on the line? Would they even care if she did?

They seemed friendly enough, but they really didn't know her. And when it was all said and done, when Tex Byrd called them all together and had his say, they'd probably head back to wherever it was they hailed from and never hear from each other again. So she couldn't very well expect them to feel any family loyalty or be inclined to do her any favors.

Or would they?

Aw, heck. Just toss it right out there, Tammy Kay. Tell 'em that you're in need of a little help learning how to apply makeup and to style your hair in something other than a braid or a ponytail.

Maybe they'd even agree to go shopping with her for a dress. Her heart spun at the possibility of doing something other women did all the time—going to stores, trying on clothes and taking part in a little girl talk. Then going home and dolling up for the first time in her life.

But it wasn't just the feminine camaraderie that she found appealing. It was the results of it that set her imagination soaring.

What if she did more than catch Doc's eye? What if he went so far as to ask her out on a date?

Her heart slipped into a zippity-do-dah beat.

But for the life of her, she couldn't seem to do anything other than spear a chunk of potato and stuff it into her mouth.

What if her cousins laughed at her, or called her a

tomboy and told her to take a hike, or refused to let her in on their secrets? Or, worse than that, if they just passed her by as if she didn't matter at all? She wouldn't bounce back from the rejection as quickly as she had in the past.

As it was, she'd be leaning on her own feminine wiles tomorrow—as scary as that was. Because, come hell or high water, she'd snag Doc's attention.

She just hoped it would be in a good way. Because going on a date with Doc Sanchez was one romantic dream she didn't want to see crash and burn.

Chapter Three

Before turning in last night, Tammy had explored the ranch house and discovered it wasn't just spacious. It was enormous.

There were two matching wings, each with four bedrooms, two of which were masters with private baths. The other two were much smaller and shared a single guest bathroom down the hall. Apparently, the girls were staying in the main wing, along with Tex.

The household help, which included Tina Crandall, the housekeeper, and Barbara Eyler, the cook, lived in the south wing in the two large rooms. Since the guest bathroom in that second wing was having plumbing problems, the men had been assigned one of several cabins within walking distance of the house.

Either way, Tammy hadn't cared where she slept… until she woke up this morning and learned that having to share a bathroom had become a real inconvenience.

Now, as she sat on the edge of the bed listening to the sound of water flowing through the pipes, she glanced again at the clock on the bureau. How much longer would she have to wait to use the shower?

Rather than twiddle her thumbs or pace the floor until the water hog finally decided to come out, she slipped into the clothes she'd been wearing yesterday and went to the kitchen, hoping she could get a cup of coffee—another of her morning habits that allowed her to start the day fresh and wide-awake.

As she crossed the living room, her bare feet padding across the hardwood floor, she savored the hearty aroma of bacon as it sizzled in a frying pan, as well as the welcome smell of fresh-brewed coffee. Her stomach growled in anticipation, so she picked up her pace.

When she entered the kitchen, she spotted Barbara standing at the counter, stirring batter in a large yellow mixing bowl.

"Good morning," Tammy said. "Do you need any help?"

The short, heavyset woman turned and smiled. "Thanks for the offer, honey, but I've got it all under control."

Back home on her father's ranch, preparing meals was Tammy's job. So it felt a little weird letting someone do all the work and serve her for a change.

"You're up early," Barbara said, as she set the batter aside.

Not really. The morning sun had already risen, so Tammy felt like a bit of a slug.

"I wanted to take a shower before coming into the

main part of the house," she said, "but someone beat me to it."

And that *someone* was taking way too long—at least ten minutes and still going strong.

If Tammy were to ever lollygag in the bathroom, she'd get chewed out—if not left behind—so she'd learned how to take quick showers. But ten whole minutes?

How in blazes could anyone have gone to bed so dirty that they needed that much soap and water?

"By the way," Barbara said, as she reached into the pantry for a bottle of oil, "your father stayed in one of the cabins last night, but he came through here about thirty minutes ago. It was good to see him again after all these years, but he didn't stick around long enough to chat. He just grabbed a cup of coffee and went back outside again. He said he was checking things out."

That's what he'd said to Tammy yesterday, but she had a feeling it was more likely that he was avoiding the house and everyone in it. But Tammy didn't see any reason to defend his actions, especially when he'd refused to let her in on any of the details of that family blowup.

"How about some coffee?" Barbara asked as she reached into the cupboard and pulled out a solid white mug.

"That sounds great. Thanks."

"How do you take it? Black?"

"Cream and sugar, please."

Barbara chuckled. "I'll never understand why people insist upon ruining a perfectly good cup of java by watering it down or doctoring it up."

The thought of doctoring anything, even a cup of

coffee, made Tammy think about Mike Sanchez, her grandfather's personal physician. There was so much she wanted to know about him, although she hated to come right out and ask. After all, she didn't want anyone to know she was…

Well, she wasn't sure what to call her curiosity and all those girlish emotions that swirled around it. She supposed she was smitten with him.

Who would have believed it?

Certainly not her father or her older brothers.

Tammy took a seat at the table and watched as Barbara prepared the coffee for her, feeling a bit like a bug on the underside of a log.

When Barbara handed her the coffee, Tammy thanked her, then took the mug, holding it with both hands and watching the steam curl up and over the rim.

Before the silence ate away at her, she asked, "How's Tex doing this morning?"

"He slept well, or so he said."

"That's good to hear." Tammy tried to think of an easy way to bring up Doc's name and slide it right into the conversation, but she really couldn't. So she'd have to work it in. "I was just wondering…I mean, I realize Tex is under a doctor's care. In fact, I met the guy yesterday, but he seemed kind of…young. You know what I mean?"

"Yes, I know exactly what you mean." Barbara stooped, opened a cupboard near the stove and pulled out a big cast-iron skillet. "But he came highly recommended from the hospital where he interned."

"Do you think he's…any good?" Tammy waited a

beat before tossing out her only real question. "What do you know about him?"

"He's definitely competent," Barbara said, "if that's what you're talking about."

No, that *wasn't* what Tammy was getting at. She wanted to know more about the man behind the stethoscope. Where did he come from? What did he do for fun?

"For what it's worth," Barbara added, "Doc Reynolds wouldn't have let anyone who didn't know his stuff cover for him while he's out getting treatment for his illness."

Tammy continued to hold her mug with both hands, weighing her words, taking care not to be too obvious. "Is Dr. Sanchez from Buckshot Hills?"

"No, he just moved here a few months ago—maybe four. He's from someplace back east. Philadelphia, I think."

Tammy took a lazy sip of coffee, relishing the sweet, creamy taste.

"Buckshot Hills is a far cry from the big city," she said.

"That's for sure." Barbara poured a splash of vegetable oil into the skillet, then turned the flame on low.

"Does he have family out here?" Tammy hoped and prayed that he didn't have a wife or a girlfriend.

"I don't think so. But to be honest, I really don't know much about him, other than Tex likes him, and he visits daily. He also seems to have a good bedside manner."

The thought of Doc standing at the side of her bed sent Tammy's thoughts hurtling in a dangerous direction. But before she could quiz the ranch cook any further, footsteps sounded in the doorway.

Tammy looked up to see Jenna entering the kitchen, fresh from the shower, her blond hair brushed in a soft, feminine style.

"Good morning," Barbara said. "Can I get you some coffee, Jenna? Or maybe some OJ? It's fresh-squeezed."

"Orange juice sounds good. Thank you, Barbara."

Tammy tried not to stare too hard at the willowy woman who was wearing jeans again today—a different pair, since they were a lighter shade of blue than the ones she'd had on yesterday.

"I know the Flying B is a cattle ranch," Jenna said, "but I noticed quite a few horses in the corral near the barn. Who takes care of them?"

"Last I heard, Caleb Granger." Barbara poured Jenna a glass of juice, then handed it to her. "Why?"

"No reason."

Barbara returned her attention to the pancakes cooking in the skillet, as if she'd thought Jenna's question had come out of the blue. But Tammy suspected there'd been a reason behind it and decided not to let it slip by the wayside.

"Do you like horses?" she asked her cousin.

"Yes, I do. In fact, I'm a certified riding instructor."

"No kidding?" Tammy sat up straight. Maybe she had more in common with her cousin than she'd thought.

Well, at least they both shared a fondness for horses, ranches and blue jeans.

"Has anything more been said about that family meeting?" Jenna asked.

"Not that I know of." Barbara used a spatula to remove several pancakes from the skillet. "I'm sure Tex will wait until everyone has arrived."

"Did my father get here yet?" Jenna asked.

"I haven't seen him." Barbara dropped a dollop of batter onto the hot skillet. "How many hotcakes do you girls want?"

"If you don't mind," Jenna said, "I'd rather have one of those leftover blueberry muffins and take it with me."

Take it *with* her?

"Where are you going?" Tammy asked her cousin.

"Just out for a walk. I'd like to see the ranch."

So would Tammy. And she was tempted to ask Jenna if she wanted company, but she held back. Her cousin had been friendly last night. And she was being nice now.

Why push herself on the woman? Tammy had learned early on how badly something like that was likely to go, how awkward. Way back in high school she'd made the mistake of approaching a popular group of girls.

She could still hear their giggles and see their smirks.

"You know," Tammy said, as she got to her feet, "I'd better take a shower now before your sister beats me to it."

"Donna's probably already showered and holed up in her room working," Jenna said. "But you never know...."

Tammy nodded, then carried her mug to the sink, not wanting to take any chances.

"I'll talk to you later," she told her cousin. "Have a nice walk."

"Thanks."

As Barbara offered Jenna a plate of muffins, Tammy returned to her bedroom for a pair of clean jeans and a shirt. Then she took them into the bathroom, which was still a little damp and steamy. After locking the door, she turned on the spigot to the shower and waited for the water to heat. As she did so, she removed her clothes.

When she was as naked as a jaybird—and a lot more womanly than most folks would guess—she stepped under the nozzle and let the water jet over her from top to bottom, wetting her hair as it hung along her back.

For a moment, she relished the warmth of the spray. Then she turned slowly, planning to reach for a bar of soap. Instead, she spotted several plastic bottles sitting on the tiled shelf inside the shower stall.

She lifted each one and read the labels, noting shampoo, conditioner and body wash.

As the water continued to sluice over her, Tammy opened each lid, taking a whiff of the girly scent of flowers.

Not bad. In fact, it was kind of nice—and certainly not her usual smell. Tammy showered as often as the next person, but she always used the generic stuff.

Unable to help herself, she squeezed out a dab of shampoo, then applied it to her wet head, hoping her cousin wouldn't mind.

As she rinsed the long, silky strands, she wondered if she ought to skip the rubber band and wear her long hair loose today.

Sure. Why not?

After she rinsed and dried off, she put on her clean clothes. Then she opened the bathroom door and allowed the dry air to chase away the steam.

Once she could see herself in the mirror again, she spotted a familiar yet very different woman staring back at her, her facial expression revealing how uneasy she felt at the unmasking.

But why wouldn't she be? Tammy had never known her mama, so she'd grown up in a man's world, making her way the best she could. And up until today—or rather, *yesterday*—she'd been happy with the strides she'd made.

But not now. Not when being a lady seemed more important than it ever had before—and far more important than trying to prove herself equal to the men in her family.

She stooped and opened the cupboard under the sink and found a handheld blow-dryer, which was still warm from use. She wondered if Jenna would mind if she borrowed it. But since Jenna had gone outside to explore the ranch, Tammy couldn't very well ask her permission.

Again she gave in to temptation. Her brush was in her purse in the bedroom, so she used her hands to dry and style the soft curls. When she'd done the best she could, she looked over her work. She definitely saw an improvement. But would it be enough?

Maybe she ought to talk to Jenna as soon as she returned from her walk. If her cousin agreed to give her a few pointers about hair—and even clothes or makeup—Tammy would feel a lot more confident when Doc arrived.

And then maybe she'd snag his attention and put a few stars in his eyes, too.

* * *

It was almost eight o'clock in the morning when Mike left town and drove out to the Flying B. He hadn't meant to visit Tex until late this afternoon, but he'd had second thoughts on his way back to the office yesterday and had decided to return earlier than he'd planned.

Tex hadn't gone into any detail about the old family feud, but Dr. Reynolds had told Mike about the old man's insistence upon making things right before he passed. And in Tex's condition, the stress of meeting new family members during an emotional and trying time could end up being too much for him.

Mike wouldn't allow himself to get personally involved with any of the Buckshot Hills residents. After all, he'd only be in town long enough to do his job and to pay his debt to his benefactor. Then he would fly home to Philadelphia, where he hoped the position with the Riverview Medical Group was still available.

But in spite of his determination to maintain a professional distance from the locals, Mike couldn't help sympathizing with Tex Byrd. The man was dying—and he wouldn't last much longer.

If Tex lived someplace else, in a bigger town or a city where hospice was readily available, Mike would have set it up the first day he'd looked over the old man's chart.

Yet it wasn't the rancher's terminal diagnosis that caused Mike to feel for him. It was his resolve to set things right within his family before he died.

Had Tex called that meeting last night? If so, Mike

wondered what had happened. How was Tex faring today? Was he in more pain? Was he distressed?

As Mike turned onto the county road and headed for the Flying B, he thought about the family members who'd gathered, as well as the stragglers who'd yet to arrive yesterday afternoon.

Were they eager to put an end to the feud? Or were they more interested in the old man's will and the division of his assets?

It was hard to say. Sometimes death brought out the worst in people.

Engagement rings did that, too.

His thoughts shifted to Katrina Willis and the blowup they'd had before he'd left Philadelphia. So much for true love, he supposed. But it was probably for the best. They'd had different plans for the future.

Katrina had called him on his cell phone last night, telling him she'd had a change of heart and that she wanted to come out to see him in Texas, maybe even stay with him. But Mike wasn't about to agree to something like that. Katrina would hate the small-town life, and he'd be miserable if he had to listen to her complaints for the next couple of weeks.

Hell, being in Buckshot Hills was difficult enough for him. Even in his wildest dreams he'd never expected to live in a place like this—albeit temporarily.

But he shook off the thoughts. Katrina was out of the picture. Mike only had himself and his mother to worry about now.

Unlike Tex Byrd, Mike's mom didn't have any real assets to divvy up. But that didn't matter. She'd been a loving, supportive mother, and because of that, Mike's childhood had been happy.

He might have grown up poor and somewhat disadvantaged—at least, until she'd gone to work for George Ballard and their financial situation had improved—but once he'd seen the good life, first through George and then through Katrina and some of his college roommates, he was determined to create that lifestyle for himself, as well as for his mother, who'd worked her tail off to raise him on her own. She deserved to finally retire and do some of the things she'd only dreamed about in the past, and Mike would soon be able to provide them for her.

Well, that is, he'd provide them once he got out of Buckshot Hills.

Up ahead, he spotted Flying B Road and reached for his turn signal. He sure hoped his patient was holding up okay—and that the plans to set things right within the family hadn't blown up in his face.

After Tammy had dried her hair, leaving it in a wild array of curls, she pondered the idea of going outside to look for Jenna. She'd gotten as far as the wraparound porch, but had chickened out and returned to the house.

As a teenager, she'd learned not to let the girls—or the boys, for that matter—know that she felt the least bit insecure about anything.

And something told her becoming an adult hadn't changed things very much.

So instead, she went back into the living room and headed down the hall until she reached the entrance to Tex's room. For the longest time, she stood at the door, her hand poised to knock, fear and pride holding her back.

Would she be out of line approaching him before he'd asked to see her?

Oh, what the heck. She rapped lightly a couple of times, then waited until an old man's voice said, "Come in. It ain't locked."

Tammy turned the knob, then entered the large bedroom where a long, lanky man lay on the bed, his face craggy, his head of thick white hair propped up on several pillows.

"I…uh…" She bit down on her bottom lip, then pressed on. "I hope I'm not bothering you, sir. But I was eager to meet you, and I thought I'd introduce myself."

"You must be Tammy, William's daughter."

She admitted she was, then eased closer to the bed. "How did you know who I was? There are three of us girls here."

He gave a little shrug. "I have my ways of keeping tabs on my boys and their families."

So what exactly *did* he know about them? Or, more specifically, about *her*?

"Don't just stand there, girl." He pointed toward the chair near his bed. "Have a seat."

"All right."

After doing as he asked, she decided to take the bull by the horns by coming right out and quizzing him about the family rift.

Before she could get the words out, he said, "You're a pretty little thing, Tammy."

No one had ever called her pretty before. Sure, they

mentioned her expressive eyes and praised the color. But *pretty?* No way.

"You look a lot like your grandma did," he said. "Her hair was dark like yours. And her eyes were nearly the same shade of blue."

"Do you have any photographs of her?" Tammy asked, curious about the woman and wondering if her look-alike had really been pretty. "If you do, I'd like to see them."

"I don't have as many as I would have liked, but I'll make sure you get at least one or two to keep." He gazed at Tammy for a moment, and a slow, wistful smile crossed his face, softening the wrinkles. "Ella Rose was a tomboy, too."

"A cowgirl, you mean?"

"I suppose so. But that little woman could turn a man inside out with a single smile. And it didn't matter if she was wearing denim or silk."

Tammy might have been more impressed with the woman's skill as a cowgirl if she hadn't just met a man who'd been able to turn *her* inside out with a smile.

"Your grandma died when the twins were in kindergarten," Tex added.

The *twins?* She'd known her father had a brother, but she hadn't realized they'd shared the same birthday. Dang. Didn't twins have some kind of weird, psychic connection, even when separated at birth?

If so, then the one William Travis and Sam Houston Byrd shared must be faulty.

Before she could comment or press Tex for more details, a couple of light knocks sounded at the door.

Her grandfather shifted in his bed, then grimaced. "Who is it?"

"Mike Sanchez."

Doc? Tammy's heart dropped to the pit of her stomach with a thud, then thumped and pumped its way back up where it belonged.

"Come on in," Tex said.

Thank goodness her grandfather issued the invitation because she couldn't have squawked out a single word, let alone managed to get up and open the door herself.

As Doc entered the room, looking even more handsome than he had yesterday, Tammy struggled to remain cool and calm, which was proving to be darn near impossible.

And it wasn't just her heartbeat going wacky. Her feminine hormones had begun to pump in a way they'd never pumped before.

"Good morning," Doc said, his gaze landing first on Tex, then on Tammy.

She managed to return his smile, although she had no idea how, when her pulse rate was so out of whack.

As he approached the bed, he continued to look at Tammy, his head cocked slightly.

"What's the matter?" she asked.

"I'm sorry. It's just that your eyes are an interesting shade of blue. I'm sure you hear that all the time."

"Not really." And not from anyone who'd ever mattered. In truth, they were a fairly common color—like the sky or bluebonnets or whatever. "I've always thought of them as run-of-the-mill blue."

"There's nothing ordinary about it. In fact, it's a pretty shade."

The compliment set her heart on end, even though it would have been nice if he'd actually said that *she* was pretty. That her hair looked especially nice today, hanging down, loose on her shoulders.

Instead, he said, "If you don't mind stepping out of the room, I'd like to examine your grandfather."

Of course she minded leaving. She wanted to stay in the same room with Doc for the rest of her natural born days. But she understood her grandfather's need for privacy.

"Of course." She got to her feet, then looked at the doctor as though he might change his mind and ask her to stay.

But he didn't. He turned back to Tex, his demeanor strictly professional.

Apparently, it was going to take more than a change of hairstyle to woo him, but there was no way Tammy would be able to pull that off by herself. And something told her that neither the housekeeper nor the cook, who were both in their sixties, would be much help in the man-wooing department.

So that left her beautiful cousins.

She had no idea what to say the next time she ran in to them. But somehow, by hook or crook, she'd have to think of something.

Because she was going to risk untold humiliation and embarrassment by begging them to turn a cowgirl into a lady.

Chapter Four

While Doc examined her grandfather in private, Tammy made her way to the living room, where she planned to hang out until she could return to Tex's room.

She had to admit that she was curious about Grandpa Tex, as well as Ella Byrd, the grandmother she supposedly favored, and the family feud. But more than that, she wanted to see Doc before he returned to his office in town. He had to be the best-looking man in all of Texas, and she stood to lose him to another woman, one who had more feminine wiles than she did.

Her heart ached at the thought, but she'd be darned if she'd just stand by and let it happen.

She might be completely out of her league when it came to competing for his affections, but it didn't matter. She did all the doctoring on her father's ranch, so they had a lot in common. All she had to do was talk to him a bit longer.

He'd mentioned the color of her eyes today, and that had to be a good sign, didn't it? He'd definitely noticed her.

Maybe she didn't need to approach Jenna about a makeover, after all. Laying her heart out to a woman who was little more than a stranger—no matter how much DNA they shared—could be embarrassing. All she needed was to have her cousin make light of it or find the whole thing amusing.

Maybe she could attract Doc on her own. She just had to find a way to spend more time with him.

She wasn't sure how to go about that, but if an opportunity arose, she planned to jump on it. In the meantime, she'd wait in the living room for Doc to come out—and for a chance to waylay him somehow.

As she prepared to plop down on the leather sofa, she heard voices in the formal dining room.

She didn't pay them any mind at first. Not until she heard Tina, the housekeeper, mention "Sam Byrd" and mumble something else. Tammy's curious nature might be the death of her some day, just as her brother Aidan always said it would, but she made her way closer to the arched doorway, taking care not to make any noise or draw any attention to herself.

It was Barbara who asked, "When do you think Sam will arrive?"

"Who knows? Maybe later today. I've already got his cabin cleaned and ready for him. From what I understand, William's two boys won't come until later in the week."

No, Tammy thought. It might be at least that long. Aidan and Nathan had gone on a remote fishing trip in Montana with a couple of their old college buddies. They didn't have cell service, so they wouldn't even get the message about coming to the Flying B until Thursday or Friday.

"I still have time to air out that bigger cabin near the far corral," Tina added. "The others either need some repair or are occupied by the ranch hands—and the dream cabin is boarded up."

The *dream* cabin? What in blazes was that? Tammy wondered, easing closer.

"Are you going to put William's sons together?" Barbara asked. "You could give them private quarters if you have one of the ranch hands cut the padlock and open up that dream cabin."

"No," Tina said. "I'd better leave that one locked up tight, just the way Tex wanted it after Savannah ran off."

Savannah? Tammy had never heard the name, which didn't mean much, since everything about the Flying B was new. But the fact that someone had run off was more than a little intriguing.

Tammy leaned forward, hoping to hear learn more.

"You're probably right. William's sons can share the bigger cabin." Barbara blew out a sigh. "That is, unless they're feuding, just like their father and uncle."

"Speaking of feuding," Tina said, "I wonder what'll happen when William and Sam finally meet face-to-face. I hope they'll be civil to each other—for Tex's sake."

"William and Sam were both good boys growing

up—and so personable. But they were also stubborn and competitive to a fault."

"No kidding. After all, they held a grudge for nearly thirty-five years."

"And all over a woman," Barbara added.

A woman? Tammy perked up. *The one who'd run off?*

"Did you ever meet Savannah?" Barbara asked.

"No. But I've heard about her over the years."

"Well, you'd better not mention her name while the family is here. You could end up starting World War III—or getting your walking papers."

"You're right. I'll keep my mouth shut. But what kind of woman comes home to meet her boyfriend's family, then sleeps with his twin brother?"

Oh, wow. Tammy had no idea…no wonder her father and uncle had a falling-out.

"Do you suppose it had anything to do with that feather bed?" Tina asked.

"You don't believe that silly legend, do you?"

"That the dreams of anyone sleeping on it come true? No, I'm not that superstitious."

Tammy straightened. *So that's why they called it the dream cabin.* It also has a legendary feather bed.

"Come on," Barbara said. "Quit your lollygagging, Tina. Help me pull this table apart so we can add the extension. We're going to have plenty of people to feed over the next few days."

"I don't know about that. Jenna is spending a lot of time outside, and her sister is holed up in the bedroom, typing away on her laptop or talking on her cell phone. William slips in when he thinks no one is around…."

Something tells me there'll be a lot of folks wanting to take their food to go."

"Hand me that table extension," Barbara said. "Now let it slip into place."

The next thing Tammy heard was a snap, a scrape and a grunt.

"There we go," Tina said. "What's for dinner tonight?"

When the discussion turned to pot roast, mashed potatoes and apple pie, Tammy returned to the living room, her thoughts a tumble with rumors and legends and family feuds.

Before she could take a seat and give her imagination free rein, a door opened down the hall, then snapped shut. Footsteps sounded, coming closer.

Oh, good. That had to be Doc.

She turned to the doorway. Even though she'd known who to expect, her breath caught at the sight of him, and her heart soared.

"You can go back in to see your grandfather, if you'd like."

Actually, she preferred to stand right here. But she smiled. "Thanks."

"I'll be back tomorrow."

Tammy might have rooted to the floor, gawking at him, if she hadn't awakened from her romantic stupor and realized he was leaving.

He tipped his head and offered her a smile. "Goodbye, Miss Byrd."

Tammy didn't know what to make of the formality. No one had ever called her Miss Byrd before. Did that mean he considered her more than the little girl who could outrope and outride her older brothers or their friends?

She sure hoped so, because for the first time in her life, she'd met a man she didn't want to compete with, but rather one she'd be willing to compete for. And while she appreciated his respect, she couldn't very well get romantically involved with a man who called her "Miss," so she said, "Please call me Tammy."

"All right." He offered her another smile, this one lighting his eyes, then headed for the door.

Unable to help herself, she followed him outside like that same lovesick puppy she morphed into whenever he was around. If she actually had a tail, it'd be wagging like crazy.

Did all doctors smell as good as he did? Did they all have such broad shoulders, such…

Oh, for Pete's sake. She had to get over it, but she didn't have a clue how to do that when it seemed that any teenage crushes she might have had while growing up had all been stored up until now, just waiting to bust out all over for the one man worthy of her heart.

So how could she just shake it all off?

Somehow, she'd have to find a way to keep him on the Flying B, even if it meant letting the air out of his tires or disabling his vehicle.

Okay, so she had the mechanical know-how to do something like that. Still, she wouldn't actually go that far. But, boy howdy, was she tempted to pull out all the stops when it came to this particular man and matters of the heart.

"Dr. Sanchez," she said, "can I ask you a question?"

"Of course."

"When my grandfather called us home, he told us that he was dying. How long does he have left?"

"It's hard to say. A couple of weeks. More or less. I've prescribed a narcotic, which helps keep the pain manageable."

Tammy bit down on her bottom lip. She'd never known her grandfather, and now that they'd finally met, she would hardly have the chance to spend any time with him.

Doc placed his hand on Tammy's shoulder in a gentle, compassionate way, yet his touch sparked a jolt of heat that spiraled to her core.

Her gaze was drawn to his. Emotion swirled around her, binding her to him somehow.

If she didn't have stars in her eyes when looking at him earlier, she surely had them now.

Oh, Lordy. She was falling hard and deep for the man. Before she could ponder whether he was feeling it, too, his cell phone rang, stealing him away from her.

"Excuse me." He removed his hand from Tammy's shoulder to answer. "Dr. Sanchez."

His brow furrowed as he listened to whomever was talking to him on the other end. "How many were injured?"

He paused a beat. "Are they conscious?" He glanced at his watch. "I'm at the Flying B, which isn't that far away. Don't take them to town. I'll meet you there. It shouldn't take more than ten minutes or so."

When Doc disconnected the line, his attention returned to Tammy. "There was an accident at the Snyders' ranch. A couple of hands trying to fix the roof on the barn fell through. It's not an emergency, but I need to head over there as soon as I talk to Tina about increasing Tex's medication."

"Do you want me to ride with you?" she asked. "I handle most of the first aid on my father's spread. I'd be happy to help."

"I appreciate the offer, but it's probably best if you stay here and visit with Tex." Before she could object, he turned and walked toward the kitchen.

Tammy didn't have a minute to spare. She had to convince him to take her with him. It would be an opportunity to show how helpful she could be, to show him how much they had in common.

So while he went looking for Tina, Tammy hurried outside and dashed to his truck. After making a quick scan to make sure no one saw what she was up to, she lifted the hood and unhooked a wire to the distributor cap. Then she lowered the hood and took off in search of Hugh, the ranch foreman. Once Doc realized his truck wouldn't start, she'd have a set of keys to one of the Flying B pickups handy.

Doc was going to need a ride, and Tammy was determined to drive him wherever he wanted to go.

As Mike sat behind the wheel of his pickup, he turned the ignition one last time. When nothing happened, he swore under his breath.

Thank God the injuries at the Snyder ranch weren't critical. If they had been, he would have had Life Flight pick them up and transport them to the hospital and met them there. But according to the foreman who'd called, both men were conscious. One claimed he was fine, but had abrasions and a possible broken ankle. The other had a head laceration and a dislocated shoulder.

Mike opened the driver's door, then climbed out of his truck. Before he could go in search of one of the Flying B ranch hands, Tex's blue-eyed granddaughter stopped him.

"Engine trouble?" Tammy asked.

"As a matter of fact, yes. But I don't have time to get to the bottom of it. I'm going to need a ride to the Snyder ranch."

She lifted a set of car keys. "I was just heading into town on a shopping trip, but that can wait. I'd be happy to drive you."

"Are you sure? It could take a while."

She smiled, those amazing blue eyes glimmering as if he was doing her a favor and not the other way around. "No problem at all. I'd only planned to go shopping because I'm bored. I'd much rather do something useful."

"All right, then. Thanks."

Tammy, whose long, dark hair hung over her shoulders and down her back in a glossy cascade of curls, nodded toward a beat-up, white Chevy pickup parked near the barn. "I've got the keys to that one. Come on, let's get out of here."

Five minutes later, Mike had transferred his medical bag and the supply case he always carried with him into the truck Tammy was driving. Then they'd taken off.

As they drove down the county road, headed toward Brian Snyder's place, Tammy said, "You'll have to give me directions. I'm not familiar with Buckshot Hills."

Neither was Mike. He'd been relying heavily on a

portable GPS system even though some of the back roads were graveled and technologically nonexistent. But he'd been to the Snyder ranch several times before. Brian's pregnant wife, Melanie, had suffered with morning sickness much longer than usual, so Dr. Reynolds had been stopping by regularly to provide an IV drip. And Mike had continued the treatment until the nausea had finally passed.

Fortunately, Melanie was doing much better now. In fact, she was due to deliver in about five weeks.

"Take a left at the next stop sign," Mike said.

Tammy did as he instructed. Moments later, he directed her to the long, unpaved driveway that would take them to the Snyder place.

"I really appreciate you driving me out here," Mike said.

"No problem. I've always handled the doctoring on my daddy's ranch. So helping you seems like the most natural thing in the world to do."

"Have you had first-aid classes?" he asked.

"Nothing formal. Whatever I learned was from books and on the internet. I find the whole medical field interesting. In fact, I probably should have majored in biology, but my dad needed me on the ranch. So I…well, I guess you could say I bloomed where I was planted."

"What did you end up majoring in?"

"I…uh…didn't go to college at all." She bit down on her bottom lip, then shot a glance at him. "I mean, I would have. It's just that my older brothers used to work construction during the summers whenever they were on a school break. And a couple of years ago, they got a contractor's license and started their own company, which was tough on my dad. He'd hoped that Aidan and Nathan would take over the ranch when he retired, but they weren't all that interested."

"So you stuck around to help out?"

Tammy shrugged. "I couldn't leave him alone. You know how it is."

No, Mike didn't. His old man had abandoned him and his mom nearly thirty years ago. He couldn't even remember the guy, let alone disappoint him.

When they reached the barn, where a ladder leaned against the side, Tammy pulled over and parked near a John Deere tractor. Mike grabbed his medical bag and climbed out. Then he reached in back for his supply case. He'd no more than taken a step toward forward, when a tall, lanky ranch hand approached the truck. "Thanks for coming, Doc. I'll show you where you can find Slim and Pete."

Mike followed the cowboy across the yard and to the house.

"Is Brian here?" he asked the man.

"No, he and his wife are away this weekend, visiting relatives in Austin. Our foreman, Jim Phelps, is in charge."

They entered through the mudroom, with Tammy on their heels, and continued to the kitchen, where Mike immediately spotted the two injured men. One was seated on a chair with his boot and sock off, his ankle badly bruised and swollen. The other held a bloody towel to his head.

Mike placed his case of supplies on the table and the smaller medical bag on the counter. Then he washed his hands and slipped on a pair of sterile disposable gloves before examining the men.

"Do you want me to clean that head wound?" Tammy asked.

"Yes, if you use this." Mike handed Tammy some antibacterial soap and sterile pads. "You'll need to get a pair of gloves for yourself."

Twenty minutes later, Mike had stitched the laceration on Pete's head and put his shoulder back in place. But Slim, the other ranch hand, was going to need X-rays and an orthopedic surgeon. In spite of his insistence that he'd be as good as new in a couple of days, Slim had clearly done a real number on his ankle. There was some obvious tissue damage, as well as a probable fracture that might need a few screws. So the tough guy was going to be laid up a lot longer than he realized.

"I can take Slim back to town with me," Mike said, "but I'm having engine trouble, which is why I had to catch a ride here."

"No problem," Jim Phelps, the foreman, said. "This is a worker's comp injury, so our boss's policy is for me to accompany him."

"Sounds good to me," Mike said. "And it's probably just as well. As soon as I get back to Tex Byrd's place, I'm going to call a mechanic or a tow truck."

"I can take a look at it for you," Tammy said.

Mike smiled at the woman who'd proven to be a good medical assistant. "Is there anything you can't do?"

"Not much." Tammy tucked her hands in the front pockets of her jeans and grinned. Her eyes sparkled, and he found himself studying her a little more closely than he ought to. Besides the size and pretty hue of her eyes, she had lush dark lashes and a pert nose dusted with freckles.

When he realized she was studying him, too, he tore his gaze away. For a moment, he wondered if little Tammy Byrd had a crush on him—not that he wasn't flattered. But he wouldn't be sticking around Buckshot Hills any longer than he had to. He was counting down the days until he could return to Philadelphia, although there wasn't any need to let that news get out until Dr. Reynolds returned or another doctor stepped up to take his place.

But damn, Mike thought, as he glanced back at Tammy. For a girl who seemed to cover up her femininity, she had the most amazing eyes.

"Can you hobble outside?" Jim asked Slim. "I'll get on your bad side and you can hold on to me for support."

As Doc turned away from Tammy and focused on his patient, Tammy's heart soared.

He'd *noticed* her. He'd truly noticed her. No man had ever looked at her like that. Maybe she wouldn't need her cousins' help and feminine advice, after all.

As the foreman helped Slim out of the kitchen, Doc packed up his supply case and medical bag. "Thanks for your help, Tammy."

"You're welcome. It was fun to see you in action. You're not only medically skilled, you're also good with people. That's got to come in handy when you doctor folks."

"Thanks. But practicing medicine in a small Texas town is a lot different than it is in the city. I'm not used to making house calls and working out of a truck. And it's frustrating to know that I don't have any high-tech labs and specialty hospitals nearby."

Tammy could understand that, but she was glad he'd come to Buckshot Hills. Otherwise, she never would have met him.

As she and Doc left the house, they spotted the foreman helping Slim get into a faded-blue Dodge pickup.

Minutes later, after Doc put his supply case in the pickup bed and climbed into the passenger seat with his medical bag, Tammy slid behind the wheel and started the engine. Then they were on their way to the Flying B.

"It's too bad you didn't go to college," Doc said. "You would have made a great doctor or nurse—if you'd wanted to."

The compliment made her heart leap, yet it also reminded her that he was a lot more educated than she was, that they didn't have as much in common as she'd hoped. Yet in spite of the momentary insecurity that whispered through her, it didn't seem to matter all that much. Not when she'd caught his eye.

"Any chance you could go back to school?" he asked.

"I doubt it."

"Would you like to?"

For some reason, whenever Tammy was around Dr. Mike Sanchez, she wasn't sure about anything anymore. So she shrugged and said, "Yes, but it's too late."

"It's never too late."

He might be right about returning to school. And she might even be tempted to look into a night class or something. But there was something else a lot more pressing right now.

Once she got back to the Flying B, she had to figure out a way to reattach that disconnected wire to the distributor cap before Doc realized what she'd done.

Okay, so she'd been far more sly and trickier than she'd ever been before. And if truth be told, all that sneakiness didn't sit too well with her. But it had been worth it just to see him gaze at her, to have him tell her what a good assistant she'd been.

Tammy stole a glance across the seat at her handsome passenger. "As soon as I get you back to the ranch, I'm going to ask you to sit behind the wheel of your truck. Then I'll lift the hood and have a little look-see. I'll bet that I can have you up and running in no time at all."

"I hope you're right. I need to get back to the office."

Knowing the raised hood would prevent Doc from seeing what she was doing and feeling a bit smug about being so clever, Tammy smiled inwardly all the way back to the ranch.

That is, until she pulled the pickup next to his truck and spotted the hood already up—and one of the Flying B ranch hands bent over the engine.

Uh-oh.

Her heart dropped to the pit of her stomach, and her cheeks warmed. If her secret got out, she was going to lose Doc before she even had a chance to win his heart.

"Hey," Doc said. "It looks as if a Good Samaritan is trying to fix my truck."

So it appeared. Tammy's heart pounded against her chest as if it wanted to break free and skedaddle before the truth hit the fan, splattering her guilt everywhere.

The ranch hand slammed down the hood, just as

Tammy parked. The blond, shaggy-haired cowboy brushed his hands together, then moseyed up to Doc's side of the truck.

Preparing for the worst, Tammy shut off the ignition. She didn't know who the ranch hand was—just that his name was Caleb something-or-other. She'd seen him around a few times. He and Hugh, the foreman, seemed to be close. She'd overheard them chuckling about something once, just like old friends sharing a joke.

But there wasn't anything funny going on now.

"My truck wouldn't start," Doc told Caleb.

"Yeah, I heard Tammy asking Hugh for the keys to one of the ranch pickups. And then I saw her drive off with you. I figured you had engine trouble."

"I didn't have time to check under the hood," Doc said, "so I appreciate you looking at it for me. Did you find out what was wrong?"

If Tammy were a coward, she might have taken off with her tail between her legs about that time, but as it was, she took the consequences of her actions like… Well, like a man, she supposed, although something about that thought rubbed her the wrong way.

"One of the wires to the distributor came loose."

Doc stiffened. "How did that happen?"

Tammy's cheeks warmed. Instead of dropping her chin, she raised it, prepared to face the consequences of her actions—if need be.

"Either someone disconnected it," Caleb said, "or it just came apart on its own."

"How could it have come loose?" Doc asked, his brow furrowed.

Caleb glanced at Tammy, who must have flushed a deep shade of okay-I-confess red. She expected him to voice his suspicion, but, instead, he just got an expression on his face as if he was either biting back a grin or a frown. She didn't know him well enough to decide which it was.

Tammy was about to suggest that the wire might have come unhooked on its own, but decided she was better off accepting the free ride the cowboy Good Samaritan seemed to be offering her.

"Well, it's fixed now," Caleb said.

Yes, and Tammy didn't have to resort to trickery to do it herself. She ought to count her blessings for that, but a surge of guilt rose up inside, taking the edge off her relief.

Should she admit to what she'd done? What harm had there been in it? Doc hadn't lost but a minute or two in getting to the Snyder ranch, and he'd said the injuries weren't serious.

They'd made such a nice step forward today that she didn't want to risk it. Maybe one day, when she and Doc were married with a passel of kids, she'd tell him what she'd done and they'd laugh about it.

Oh, for Pete's sake. Who was she kidding? A romance between her and Doc didn't stand a chance of blossoming unless Tammy did something to close the gap in their differences—and fast.

But how would she go about doing that? She wasn't in a position to sign up for any online college courses while she was at the Flying B, so she'd have to do the next best thing.

She'd have to throw herself at her cousins' feet and beg for their help—no matter what their reactions might be.

Chapter Five

Tammy had hoped to talk to her cousins over dinner last night, but from what Barbara had told her, Jenna had gone into town earlier, saying she'd be back late. And Donna had holed up in her room again, working on some project. So even though Tammy had been primed to broach the subject of helping her, the girl-talk had to wait until breakfast.

But the next day, after the sun came up, Tammy found herself seated alone at the kitchen table once more.

"Where's Jenna?" Tammy asked the cook.

"You just missed her. She had an early breakfast and went for a walk."

Tammy didn't even bother asking about Donna, who kept herself pretty scarce.

So how in blazes was Tammy supposed to ask either of them to give her some feminine hints?

She glanced at the clock on the stove. She still had several hours to learn how to put on a little makeup, since Doc probably wouldn't arrive until afternoon. So she wasn't going to worry about it.

In the meantime, she had plenty to keep herself busy until then. As soon as she finished the last of her coffee, she was going to set out on a fact-finding mission.

Last night, after dinner, she'd quizzed Barbara. Instead of admitting that she'd eavesdropped on a private conversation, she told her she'd been on a walk and had stumbled upon a cabin that had been locked up. When she'd asked the cook about it, Barbara had said, "I have no idea," making it clear that she wouldn't spill the beans about Savannah.

But maybe one of the ranch hands would. Still, even if Tammy came up empty-handed in the gossip department, she planned to find that cabin and do some snooping.

Not that she believed there was anything magical about the bed. After all, Tammy might be as curious as the proverbial dead cat, but she wasn't superstitious. Still, she was determined to find the cabin and check it out. So after rinsing her plate and coffee cup in the sink, she went outside and scanned the yard.

The only ranch hand she spotted was Caleb, the one whose good deed had nearly thrown Tammy's soaring romantic plans into a tailspin yesterday.

"Hey," she said, as she approached the cowboy.

"What's up?" he asked.

"I wanted to thank you for not accusing me of disconnecting that wire yesterday."

"Did you?"

"I hate to admit it, but yes. I did."

Caleb arched an eyebrow. "Why in the hell did you do that?"

Was he angry with her? Tammy wasn't sure, because there was a trace of amusement in his question.

"I had my reasons," she said.

"And what if Doc would have had an emergency?"

"I was ready to drive him wherever he needed to go."

Caleb crossed his arms and eyed her carefully, a grin emerging. "Don't tell me you took a fancy to Doc Sanchez."

Her first impulse was to deny it, but Caleb hadn't squealed on her when he had the chance, and something told her he might prove to be a good friend—or at least an ally. And if there was something she'd learned about herself, it was that she could use someone in her corner every now and again.

"Yes, I'm attracted to him, but he hardly knows I'm alive."

Caleb sketched a gaze over her, his expression softening into a full-blown smile that dimpled his cheeks. "Well, you're pretty enough. But you certainly don't do anything to stand out from the female crowd."

She could defend herself, but why? Caleb probably wouldn't understand. She studied him for a moment in the morning light, making a quick visual assessment of him, just as he'd done to her.

He was nice-looking—and maybe a bit charming—but he didn't appeal to her in the same heart-strumming way that Doc did. And she found that more than a little interesting. Apparently, chemistry, pheromones and sexual attraction were not just amazing, they were also unpredictable.

Tammy shook off her thoughts and focused on the problem at hand. "Can I ask you a question?"

Caleb, who carried a tool belt cinched to his waist, crossed his arms. "Sure."

"Do you know anything about the dream cabin?"

He furrowed his brow. "Are you talking about the one that Tex locked up years ago?"

She nodded.

"Not really."

By the way he said it, Tammy wasn't sure if he was telling the truth or not. Either way, she sensed he was holding something back.

"Which one is it?" she asked. There were quite a few cabins scattered on the property, some of which housed ranch hands—maybe even Caleb.

The cowboy didn't respond right away, and she wondered if he was deciding whether he wanted to dole out any information or not. Finally, he lifted his arm and pointed to the east. "It's the farthest one from the house. Since I'm going to check on the pump at the old well, which is near there, I'll show you."

"Thanks." Tammy couldn't ask for more than that.

As Caleb began walking, Tammy strode along beside him.

"Why did you want to know about that cabin?" he asked.

"Just curious." As their boots crunched along the dirt path, Tammy asked, "What do you know about it?"

"Well, apparently there's an antique feather bed inside that some folks think is magical."

"Really?"

Caleb laughed. "You mean, do people really make that claim? Or that dreams come true?"

"That people think there's something to the legend, I guess. You don't believe it?"

"Of course not. But Ella, Tex's late wife, did."

"Where'd the bed come from?"

"It used to belong to Tex's mother, who claimed to have the gift of sight—or something like that. And Ella was uneasy about the whole thing. So once the old woman passed on, Ella demanded that Tex get the bed out of the house. And he had it moved to the farthest cabin on the ranch."

"That's why the door is locked?"

Again Caleb paused, but this time he merely shrugged. But Tammy wasn't appeased.

"Did it have anything to do with Savannah?"

Caleb slowed to a stop, then turned and crossed his arms. "What about her?"

The handsome ranch hand was too young to have known Savannah personally, but clearly he'd heard of the woman—whoever she was.

"Who was she?" Tammy asked.

Caleb chuffed. "Who really knows? Savannah's about as legendary as that fool bed."

"What do you mean?"

"I've only heard rumors, so I'm not going to repeat them or speculate. You'll have to get your scoop from someone else."

As Caleb started toward an old pump, which was about fifty yards to the east, Tammy hiked to the knoll and beyond to the lone cabin, with its rickety but quaint porch.

Bushes and shrubs grew wild along the exterior walls, and as Tammy approached the entrance, she caught the scent of honeysuckles. She was half tempted to pluck a blossom, but instead, she climbed the single step to the porch.

The door had been secured with a rusted padlock. And the front window had been boarded up. At one time, the cabin might have been a happy place, with gingham curtains and a pot of geraniums at the door. But after nearly thirty-five years of neglect, it appeared sad and forlorn.

Undaunted at being locked out, Tammy slipped around to the back of the cabin, checking for another way inside.

She spotted a back door, which was also boarded up. But just as she'd hoped, she found a window. It, too, had been boarded up at one time, although a couple of the slats had come loose. Tammy tugged at one of them, and with very little effort, managed to remove it. The others came off just as easily.

How was that for luck?

As she peered through the dusty, grimy glass, she couldn't see much—just the legendary bed, a single nightstand and a bureau.

As she tried to open the pane, the latch gave way.

"Hot damn," she said, realizing she was in luck. But she was going to have a difficult time climbing up that high without a boost or something to step on. So she scanned the yard.

Near a sycamore tree, she spotted an old battered

bucket nearly covered by overgrown grass. So she went after it and placed it upside down against the wall. Then, using it as a step, she pulled herself through the window, scraping her tummy on an old nail while she was at it.

"Ow," she cried out before catching herself. Caleb wasn't that far away, and she didn't want him to know what she was doing—although he'd probably guessed.

Her belly stung from the scrape, but she ignored it as she climbed down into the small, dusty bedroom. Her presence alone seemed to stir up the dust. Her nose itched, and she sneezed twice.

Boy, did this place need a good cleaning.

Nevertheless, she made her way to the legendary antique bed. She didn't believe any of the claims of magic, but she felt something, just being inside the cabin.

Or maybe she was just getting a *feel* for the woman who'd once lived here.

Unable to help herself, she went to the bureau and opened the drawers, finding them all empty. Next she checked the nightstand, which held a couple of books, one of which was a small cookbook entitled *Romantic Dinners for Two*.

Tammy took a seat on the feather mattress and scanned the pages filled with pictures of various candlelit table settings and a slew of menu ideas. Since she'd done all the cooking on her dad's ranch, she'd become a pretty good cook, if she did say so herself. And some of the recipes looked pretty darn tempting.

She imagined bringing Doc out to the cabin for a romantic dinner, but she'd probably have to hogtie him first. She'd also have to spend hours scrubbing the place, but since her brothers wouldn't be arriving until Sunday, she had plenty of time on her hands.

But before she could plan anything romantic, she had to find her cousins and convince them to help with a makeover—even if it was just a quick lesson in applying lipstick and mascara.

So she shoved the books back into the nightstand drawer, then returned to the open window and began her climb down. But when her denim jeans snagged and caught on the nail, throwing her off balance, she fell to the ground with a rip and a thump.

Pain shot through her shoulder, which took the brunt of her weight, and she wondered if she'd broken something.

Aw, man. This was going to be hard to explain....

Caleb, who'd apparently seen her take the tumble, rushed over to her. "Are you okay?"

Never one to let any of the men know when she was hurting, she scrunched her face and tried to bite back the tears.

Caleb placed his hand on her injured shoulder, which hurt like a son of a gun, and she winced. "Never mind," he said. "Let me help you up. Then I'll drive you into town and let Doc check you out."

Tammy opened her mouth to object, but when she thought about walking into Doc's clinic, having him examine her and offer some TLC...

Well, heck. She may as well milk her injury for all it was worth.

Even though Mike spent a lot of time making house calls to various ranches in the area, he still kept office hours at the small clinic in town. And today was no different.

According to the list Eleanor Watkins, his receptionist, had given him when he'd arrived this morning, he had several appointments scheduled between ten and noon, but nothing sooner.

So he poured himself a cup of the coffee Eleanor had just brewed, then went back to his cramped office in the rear of the clinic, where he took a seat at his desk and began to look over the lab reports that had just come in.

He'd no more than picked up the first one when his cell phone rang. He was so focused on the results before him that he answered without first checking the lighted display.

"Mike?" a familiar voice sounded. "It's me, Katrina."

He didn't respond right away, but not just because he hadn't expected his former fiancée to call him again.

"Hey," he said, surprised at how casual he sounded. "How's it going, Kat?"

This time, Katrina was the one to let a couple of beats pass before answering.

"Not so good," she finally said. "Philadelphia isn't the same without you."

He'd hoped she would have come to that conclusion before he'd left, but she hadn't. In fact, when he'd suggested she come to Buckshot Hills with him so they could be together, she'd refused to even consider a temporary move or even regular visits. Her life, she'd told him, was in Philadelphia. And while he understood she was a city girl through and through, he'd kind of hoped her "life" would have been with him.

"When are you coming back to civilization?" she asked.

Mike was torn between defending the folks in Buckshot Hills and admitting that a part of him was eager to return to Philadelphia and to all the city had to offer.

"It could be another month or two," he said. "Maybe longer. It all depends upon how Dr. Reynolds's treatment goes."

"That's not so long, I suppose."

Mike leaned back in his chair. That was another conclusion he'd wished she'd come to earlier. But she hadn't, and knowing that she hadn't been willing to sacrifice her comfort so they could be together, even temporarily, had hurt. And he'd had to reconsider making a lifetime commitment to her, no matter how much she claimed to love him. Or how much he'd thought he loved her.

Sure, there were still feelings involved—both ways. But he'd fought too long and too hard to achieve a medical degree and to make a place for himself in a social circle that hadn't always been open to him. And now that he had, he wasn't going to let anyone try to map out his future—even Katrina. And that's what she'd been trying to do ever since the start of their relationship.

As he was ending his residency, she'd urged him to accept a position with a renowned medical group that specialized in plastic surgery, even though she'd known that he would have preferred a more traditional practice. And when she found out that he'd felt an obligation to cover for Dr. Reynolds for a few months, she'd flipped out, setting their breakup in motion.

"In the scheme of life," Mike said, "a few months really isn't that long, Katrina."

Just long enough to miss out on a medical opportunity of a lifetime, though. And while Katrina hadn't been wrong for pointing that out when it had come time for Mike to repay his debt to George Ballard, she hadn't understood that Mike owed the wealthy man more than just the cost of his med school tuition.

George had gone above and beyond for Mike's mom, too. And some kindnesses could never be repaid.

Mike had tried to explain this to Katrina when they'd talked over his decision to go to Buckshot Hills. She hadn't understood at the time, but now she seemed to be having second thoughts.

"I miss you," she said. "I just wanted you to know that."

His bruised ego liked hearing it. Was she going to tell him again that their breakup had been a big mistake, that she was sorry she'd been so hasty in letting him go?

But even more important, would that change anything?

He wasn't sure. And he wasn't about to commit one way or another. After all, it had taken her nearly four months to come to that conclusion.

Or was it merely the fact that she realized he'd be returning to Philly soon, and that she was hoping they could take up right where they'd left off?

He glanced at the clock on the wall of his office. It was 9:05 a.m. in Texas, an hour later on the east coast. He didn't expect a patient to come in for nearly an hour. Still, he didn't feel like poking at old wounds—or creating new ones and merely said, "I appreciate the call, Katrina."

"I know you're busy now, honey, so I'll let you go. I'll call back later. Probably this evening."

He could have admitted that he wasn't all that busy now, but it seemed as if he was the one needing some space and time to sort things out.

"All right," he said. "Have a good day, Kat. I'll talk to you later."

The line had no more than disconnected when a light rap sounded. The only one in the office, as far as he knew, was his receptionist/office manager. "Come on in, Eleanor."

The door swung open, and the matronly woman poked her head inside. "Dr. Sanchez, Tex Byrd's granddaughter had an accident on the Flying B. One of the hands just brought her in. I put her in the exam room."

Oh, no. His gut clenched. He had no idea which girl it was—hopefully not Tammy. But either way, the poor family didn't need any other complications.

"I'll be right there," Mike said, as he set the lab reports aside, rolled back his chair and stood. Then he headed down the short hall.

When he stepped into the small exam room, he spotted Tammy seated on the table. She was wearing a flannel shirt and a pair of jeans that had a jagged tear at the knee. Her hair was a bit windblown and had a leaf stuck in the strands.

"Tammy?" he asked with concern. "What happened?"

"I…" Her cheeks, one of which bore a smudge of dirt, flushed. "I took a tumble."

"Off a horse?"

"Actually, I…" She bit her lower lip, then gave a little shrug. "I fell out of a window."

Tammy was one of a kind—a real novelty, it seemed. And he couldn't help but grin. "Pray tell, what were you doing? Climbing in or out?"

"Out."

"Was there a reason you didn't use the door?" His smile broadened, as he neared the exam table.

"It was locked, and I didn't have a key."

"Why doesn't that surprise me?"

She gave another shrug, then winced.

He eased closer to the exam table. "What hurts?"

She lifted her right arm and pointed to her left shoulder.

"Okay, let's get that shirt off of you so I can check your injury."

As Tammy began to reach for the top button, her fingers struggled.

"Here," he said. "Let me."

Mike unbuttoned her shirt, then carefully pulled the fabric back, revealing…

Oh, wow. Tammy Byrd might look like a rough-and-tumble cowhand on the outside, but underneath…? She was definitely all woman.

He shook off the completely inappropriate and unprofessional thoughts and focused on her shoulder, on the slight abrasion, on the…

…softness of her skin, the contours along her throat…

As he gently probed along her collarbone, he asked, "Does this hurt?"

"Not too bad. It's actually feeling much better now. I'm sure it's just a bruise, but Caleb insisted I have it checked."

"It's best to get a medical opinion when in doubt," Mike said.

After checking her mobility, which wasn't impaired, he had to agree that she'd probably just bruised her shoulder.

"I can order an X-ray if you'd like me to rule out a fracture or tissue damage," he said.

"That's probably not necessary." Tammy began to tug on the flannel shirt, hiding her femininity once more. Again, when it came time to button, she struggled.

"Let me."

"Thanks."

Again, Mike had to shake off his inappropriate thoughts, telling himself that his interest had been piqued by the surprise of it all—and nearly buying in to it.

Once she was completely buttoned up, he stepped back to make a note in her chart. "You can take some aspirin or acetaminophen for the pain and ice it when you get home. If you take it easy for a day or two, you should feel better soon. And if not, give me a call."

"I will. Thanks, Doc." Tammy smiled, those amazing blue eyes glimmering with…what? Appreciation? Respect? Maybe even a bit of adoration?

Mike had no idea what was going on in her mind, but something told him her wheels and cogs were turning. And he wasn't sure what that meant. After all, the woman had been climbing in and out of windows on the ranch. He wouldn't put much past her.

"Thanks, again," Tammy said, as she began to climb from the exam table.

"Here." Mike reached out his hand. "I don't want you falling again."

But when he touched her, an unexpected jolt of heat surged through him, and it took a moment to recover. What was that all about?

As she walked out of the room, Doc watched her go. There was something interesting about Tammy. Something...intriguing.

He'd actually had an arousing reaction to the cowgirl, although, under the exterior, she was woman through and through.

But after his breakup with Katrina nearly four months ago, Mike wasn't interested in romance. And even if he were, it certainly wouldn't be with a small-town tomboy who would never fit into Philadelphia society. Hell, it had taken Mike long enough to do that himself, and he'd at least grown up around it, even if he'd never been a part of it back then.

Still, after returning to his office, he found himself at the window, peering outside and watching Tammy climb into the passenger seat of one of the ranch pickups.

And imagining what she might look like if she'd removed the denim as well as the flannel.

On the way back to the ranch, Tammy couldn't help the smile that stretched across her face.

While Doc had examined her, when he'd caught a

glimpse of the real Tammy, the part of her she usually kept under wraps, his breath had caught, and his voice had grown soft and husky. She wasn't at all experienced when it came to romance or things of the heart, but there was definitely something sexual going on between them.

"I'm sorry for insisting that you see the doctor when your injury didn't turn out to be serious," Caleb said. "But I figured it was better to be safe than sorry."

"Don't be sorry." Tammy had been thrilled to have an excuse to see Doc again. And just knowing that he'd seen her as a real woman was worth any effort it took to get to the clinic or any charge for an office visit. "You're absolutely right about not taking chances."

As they continued down the road awhile, Tammy thought about Doc and her plan to reveal even more of the true woman inside—and not just the physical part. Trouble was, she couldn't quite get a handle on how to go about it.

She glanced across the cab at Caleb, saw him just as deep in thought, his hands gripping the steering wheel, his gaze on the road, his mind clearly somewhere else.

"What's the matter?" Tammy asked. "Is something wrong?"

"Not really."

She didn't quite believe him, although she probably didn't have the right to pry.

"I owe you for driving me into town," Tammy said. "I'm a pretty good cook, since I prepared all the meals on my dad's ranch. So while I'm here, I'll ask Barbara if she'll let me borrow the kitchen long enough to make you some brownies or chocolate chip cookies."

Tammy would make a big enough batch to give some to Doc, too. Didn't they say the way to a man's heart was through his stomach? And Tammy was a pretty darn good cook—even if most folks didn't know it.

"You don't owe me anything," Caleb said. "Besides, I'm going to be leaving soon."

"Leaving?"

Caleb's grip on the wheel loosened, and when he glanced at Tammy, his expression softened. "Well, not for good. I'll be back. I have to settle a few family matters, so I'm just taking a leave of absence."

Tammy could understand that. The Byrds had a few things to settle, too—like the rift between her dad, her uncle and her grandfather that had gone on way too long.

They continued to ride in silence. Tammy's thoughts drifted from family issues to matters of the heart. She'd had a crush on one of her brothers' friends while she was growing up, but what she was feeling for Dr. Mike Sanchez was bigger, stronger and far more compelling.

In fact, she was going to have to do something about it before the yearning to kiss him darn near killed her.

As Caleb pulled into the yard and parked near the house, Tammy spotted Jenna standing near the corral, stroking the neck of a roan gelding. As soon as Caleb shut off the ignition, Jenna strode toward the pickup, just as Tammy was getting out.

"Hugh mentioned that you fell and got hurt," Jenna said to Tammy. "Are you all right?"

"I'm okay. It's nothing serious."

The front door opened, and Donna stepped out of the house. She made her way down the porch steps and across the yard. Worry and concern marred her cover-girl face.

Well, what do you know? Tammy seemed to be making friends with her cousins without much effort.

She turned to Caleb, who was standing next to her. The cowboy was looking at Donna as though she was the prettiest little filly he'd ever seen.

Was Caleb having a love-at-first-sight moment, just as Tammy had experienced when she first laid eyes on Doc? If so, she felt sorry for him since Donna didn't appear to have noticed.

But what did Tammy know about romance? She was a complete novice at that sort of thing, so she probably ought to keep her observation to herself.

When she glanced again at Caleb, he'd already started in the direction of the main barn. Was he bummed by Donna's brush-off? Or was he caught up in the family issues he was going home to settle?

Probably the family stuff.

Gosh, Tammy hoped they weren't as bad as the troubles the Byrds were facing. Yet as he walked away with a sexy cowboy saunter, he didn't seem to be fazed by Donna's lack of interest.

"What happened?" Jenna asked.

"It's a long story. And it all started when I heard a rumor about a cabin that had been locked up after a woman named Savannah ran off. So I thought I'd have a look inside. But the only way to get in, short of cutting the padlock, was to go through the back window. And I…well, I fell out."

Her cousins merely glanced at each other, as though

Tammy must have landed on her noodle instead of her shoulder.

"What are you talking about?" Jenna asked.

While Tammy had been eager to ask her cousins to help with a makeover, she decided it might be best to get on their good sides first. And what better way to do that than to let them in on a little secret, even if it might be more rumor or conjecture than anything?

"From what I heard," Tammy said, "either my dad or yours had a girlfriend named Savannah. She was staying at the ranch in one of the cabins. And after she ran off, Tex locked up the place. So I thought it would be interesting to see what was inside."

"What's so intriguing about a locked-up cabin?" Donna asked.

Tammy shifted her weight to one hip. "It's not just the cabin. It's what I heard about Savannah and our fathers."

Both cousins were listening, clearly intrigued so far.

"I don't know which twin was which," Tammy said, although she had a pretty solid suspicion, especially since her father had said his brother had done something unforgivable. "One of them slept with the other's girlfriend."

Jenna furrowed her brow. "No wonder there was a blowup."

"That's awful," Donna said. "I can't believe that two brothers would sleep with the same woman."

"I don't know all the details yet," Tammy said, "but I'm going to get to the bottom of that feud if it's the last thing I do."

Both of her cousins seemed to be pondering the revelation, but Tammy kept the "unforgivable" comment to herself. At this point, she didn't want her cousins to think she was taking sides or pointing fingers.

"And guess what else?" Tammy added. "There's an old feather bed in that cabin that's become some kind of legend around here. Supposedly, the dreams people have while sleeping on it are supposed to come true."

Before either woman could comment, Donna's cell phone rang. She glanced at the display. "I'm sorry. I need to take this call." Then she stepped away, heading back to the house and leaving Tammy with Jenna.

All Tammy needed was for Jenna to find an excuse to leave before she got a chance to lay her heart—and her hopes—on the line, so she said, "I was wondering if I could ask you a favor."

"What's that?"

"Would you like to go shopping in town with me someday soon? We could, you know, have lunch, get to know each other...."

"That sounds fun," Jenna said. "I'd love to. In fact, what do you have planned for tomorrow morning?"

"Not one darn thing. Tomorrow would be perfect."

Tammy couldn't believe her luck. Did she dare tell her cousin what she was hoping to gain from the shopping trip? That she'd get some help in choosing just the right clothes to wear? Something stylish and sexy at the same time?

And that she'd get some advice on what makeup to buy, how to apply it... Goodness, there was *so* much to know, to learn.

But it would all be worth it—especially if the next time she ran in to Doc he'd see her in a whole new light.

Chapter Six

Tammy had built up a small nest egg over the years, thanks to the small salary her father paid her and no reason to spend much of it on anything in the past. So she decided not to limit herself when it came to shopping. In fact, she'd spent nearly five hundred dollars on clothes and shoes and makeup while she'd been at the mall with Jenna and would have spent more if she hadn't been afraid her cousin would think she'd gone a little crazy. But she didn't mind a bit. She loved everything she'd bought and couldn't wait to get dolled up for Doc.

All in all, it had been a great day.

She'd never had a woman to shop with before or to advise her on fashion and style. And Jenna had been such a good sport. She'd never once made Tammy feel like a bumbling fool when it came to feminine apparel. Instead, she'd complimented her hair, her eyes, her shape...

And even though Tammy had always been a bit embarrassed by her large breasts, she was actually beginning to see them as real assets now.

Okay, so having Doc clearly zero in on her womanly endowments when he'd examined her shoulder and sensing his reaction had been pretty convincing in and of itself.

When she and Jenna finally returned to the Flying B, the bags and boxes filling the cab of the ranch pickup, they saw that Doc had arrived.

Tammy's heart soared at the sight of him. He was standing near the driver's door of his truck, and she hoped that he was coming and not going.

When Jenna shut off the engine, Tammy nearly left her purchases in the truck so she could speak to Doc before he drove off or went into the house. But she didn't want to appear too eager to see him.

Instead, she reined in her enthusiasm the best she could and calmly reached for the bags.

"Here, let me get some of those," Jenna said.

"Thanks." Still, Tammy took several of the corded handles in each hand. As she shut the passenger door, Doc approached.

"I was going to ask how your shoulder was doing," he said, "but I can see that it must not be giving you too much trouble."

Tammy's cheeks warmed, but she managed to toss him a breezy smile. "Actually, Jenna's carrying the heavy stuff. But I'm doing okay. Thanks for asking."

"You're wearing makeup," he said.

Just a bit of mascara. But thank goodness he hadn't seen her before. While at one of the department stores, Tammy and Jenna had stopped by a cosmetics counter, where one of the clerks had applied all kinds of stuff to her face, making her look like a clown.

Well, Jenna hadn't agreed with that assessment. But when Tammy had peered in the mirror and seen all that stuff around her eyes and the heavy coat of red lipstick, she'd gone into the nearest ladies' room afterward and washed most of it off.

Now she wished she hadn't.

"I like it," Doc said. "It makes your eyes sparkle."

The compliment and the way he smiled at her sent her senses scampering in a hundred different directions. She managed to utter a thank-you, but she had a feeling that most of the "sparkle" came from her excitement at seeing him again.

"I'll talk to you later," he said, nodding toward the house. "I need to go inside." Then he headed for the front porch, leaving Tammy completely awestruck and speechless.

"No wonder you wanted to pick up some new clothes," Jenna said.

Huh? Tammy turned to her cousin, who sported a knowing grin. Then she blew out a sigh. "Is it that obvious?"

"You might as well be wearing a neon sign."

That's what Tammy had been afraid of. But why pretend otherwise, especially when Jenna had been so cool about the shopping trip and so fun to spend the morning with? "I hate to admit it, but I'm afraid you're right. I'm flat-out smitten with him."

"So what are you going to do about it?"

"I'm not sure. But I'd love some advice if you have any to spare. I was raised around men. So I've always felt more comfortable about them, especially when it comes to working on the ranch and shooting the breeze. But Doc is different."

Jenna smiled. "You're a beautiful woman, Tammy. All you need is a little makeover. Come on. Let's go to my room. I'll show you how easy it is to turn a cowgirl into a knockout."

"I'm not so sure about *that*. But I'd be happy to snag his attention."

Okay, so if truth be told, she wanted to snag a whole lot more than his attention. But that, she feared, would take a miracle.

Tammy followed Jenna into her bedroom, where they laid the bags and boxes on the bed.

"Why don't you slip out of those clothes," Jenna said. "We'll find a new outfit for you to wear."

As Tammy undressed, she fought the urge to cover her breasts with her arms. But Jenna didn't seem to notice her insecurity.

"Take off those granny panties and the bra, too," Jenna said, as she reached for the glossy pink bag with a gold cord handle and candy-striped tissue.

"Why?" Tammy asked. "Who's going to know what I have on underneath?"

"You are. And just the awareness of those sexy undergarments will put a sway in your steps." Jenna reached into the bag and pulled out the skimpy panties and bra she'd encouraged Tammy to purchase earlier. "Slip these on."

"Okay," Tammy said, "but I'm not sure it'll make a difference."

Minutes later, Tammy had to admit that the delicate black satin and lace made all the difference in the world.

"Dang," she said, studying her image in the mirror. "I can't believe that's me."

"And neither will Doc, even if you cover those undies with that slinky black dress we bought at Becky's Boutique."

After Tammy slipped into the garment, Jenna zipped the back. "Next comes the hair."

"We don't have time to do much with it," Tammy said. "I don't want to be fussing over myself too long. What if Doc leaves before he gets a chance to see the new me?"

"It won't take long."

With that, Jenna removed the rubber band that held Tammy's hair in a ponytail, letting it fall over her shoulders and down her back.

"While the curling iron heats, I'll fiddle with your makeup."

"Don't make me look like a clown," Tammy said. "I'd die if Doc laughed at me."

"He won't laugh. I promise."

For some reason, Tammy believed her cousin, trusting her in a way she'd never trusted another woman before.

Tammy had secretly yearned for a mother's love—or at least, to have another female around who understood why she sometimes got weepy during certain times of the month. Or why men could be so hard-headed and stubborn.

But working with her dad and brothers on the ranch didn't give her much time to make friends or to socialize, which had always been okay with her. At least, that's what she'd told herself over the years. But now she wasn't so sure.

"You know," Tammy said, "sometimes I really missed not having a sister or a mom."

Jenna reached for a tube of lipstick. "What happened to your mother?"

"She died in a car accident. My dad raised me and my two older brothers single-handedly, so I learned early on how to make it in a man's world. But I didn't realize that not having any women in my life would also leave me at a big disadvantage."

As Jenna worked her magic with the makeup, Tammy added, "Growing up on a ranch had its benefits, of course. Not many men can best me as a cowhand."

Jenna smiled. "I can see how that would happen."

Could she? Tammy wished the girls at school would have been as open-minded.

For some reason, she felt the need to share her vulnerability with Jenna, which was a real first. She usually kept things like that close to the vest. But after the time she'd spent with Jenna today—and now with the makeover—she had a feeling she could trust her cousin not to laugh or hold her struggles and insecurities against her.

"When I was a kid," Tammy said, venturing out on a shaky limb, "people called me Tam-boy." She didn't mention how badly the taunts had hurt.

Jenna stepped aside to allow Tammy a chance to sneak a peek in the mirror. "No one will be calling you that now."

Oh, wow. Tammy blinked, then studied the vaguely familiar yet stunning brunette who peered back at her. "I can't believe it. I don't even look like me anymore."

"That clerk at the makeup counter was way too heavy-handed," Jenna said. "All you need is a subtle amount to highlight those eyes and your lips. What do you think?"

"I'm amazed at the change. But are you sure I don't look like a vamp or a tramp or a seductress or..."

Jenna laughed. "Don't be silly. No one would ever mistake you for anything other than a beautiful woman with a pure heart. And Doc would have to be dead or blind not to sit up and take notice."

"Okay. Maybe you're right. But those changes are all on the outside. I'm still the same person on the inside. How do I act? What do I say?"

"Just be yourself." Jenna, who was standing behind Tammy now, caught her gaze through the mirror. Then she placed both hands on Tammy's shoulders and smiled. "Just don't sell yourself short. Get to know Doc. Make sure he's the right one for you—and that he's not just another handsome face."

"What do you mean?"

"Make sure he has all the qualities you're looking for in a man."

Jenna made it sound as if Tammy had been hunting for a boyfriend or a mate for ages, when she'd just kind of stumbled on Doc and found herself considering romance for the first time in her life.

"I never gave the whole dating thing much thought before laying eyes on Doc," Tammy admitted.

"Well, if you keep dressing like a woman instead of a cowhand, you'd better start thinking about the future—and what you're looking for in a man—because you're going to have more male attention than you can shake a stick at."

"Have you?" Tammy asked. "I mean, have you given a man's qualities much thought?"

"You bet I have. I've even made a list. And if a guy doesn't have every one of those qualities, I don't bother going out a second time."

"That's amazing." Tammy returned her cousin's grin.

"Life is too short to waste it on the wrong man."

Tammy thought about that for a moment, then broke into another grin. "I'd make a list, too, but it would just have three little words on it."

"What words would that be?"

"Doctor Michael Sanchez."

They shared a full-on laugh—two women, two friends, both on the same page. And it felt good for a change. *Darn* good. Where had this cousin been all her life? Why couldn't she have gotten to know Jenna when they were both younger?

Because of the family feud, that's why. Thank God Tex was hoping to end it all.

"Come on," Jenna said. "Let's go out in the living room. Doc will be leaving soon, and I can't wait to hear what he has to say about the new you."

Neither could Tammy. She'd give anything to turn Doc's heart on end.

And if she could manage to walk in those crazy high heels without falling flat on her face and making a complete fool of herself, she'd be over the moon.

As Mike removed his stethoscope and placed it in his medical bag, he realized Tex was growing weaker each day. He'd also need a change in his pain medication, since he'd been feeling nauseated lately, which was a side effect of the narcotic he was taking. Mike had been holding off on prescribing morphine, but he couldn't wait any longer. The man's pain was clearly getting worse.

According to Tex, the family meeting was scheduled for Sunday, when the last of his relatives—two grandsons—would be at the ranch. Mike hoped the old man would be coherent and strong enough to say all he wanted to say.

"I'll stop by and see you again tomorrow," he told the dying rancher, "but if you need anything before then, give me a call."

"I will. Thanks, Doc."

As Mike opened the bedroom door and let himself out, he headed down the long, narrow hallway. When he reached the living room, he spotted a petite brunette peering out the window and into the yard. She wore a pair of high heels and a slinky black dress that clung to her curves.

Mike drew up short. Who the heck was she? Another of Tex's granddaughters?

When she turned, facing him, recognition dawned and his jaw dropped. He didn't know who he'd expected to see on his way out of the house, but certainly not a gorgeous brunette with a shape that could stop traffic at rush hour in downtown Philadelphia.

Was that really Tammy?

Damn, it couldn't be anyone else.

"Hey," she said, offering him a shy smile. "How's Tex doing this afternoon?"

"He's…about the same." Mike tried to focus on his reason for being on the Flying B, on his patient, on re-laying medical information to the man's granddaughter. But all he could do was marvel at the new Tammy.

Not that the old Tammy, with those pretty blue eyes, hadn't been intriguing and fun to know. But who in the world left a palette of makeup out? And who opened the door to Victoria's Secret after hours? And why hadn't they done it sooner?

Tammy tucked a strand of hair behind her ear. "Is something wrong, Doc?"

"Wrong? No." Hell, no. It's just that he… Damn. "I didn't recognize you at first, and it kind of…threw me for a loop, I guess."

"It's the dress."

No, it was more than the dress—although the style and fabric certainly spotlighted the woman he'd failed to see before.

He probably ought to say something else, to com-ment about the new Tammy. But he was…dumbstruck. Awestruck. Maybe even a bit moonstruck.

Not that he'd do anything about it. Even if he were inclined to give Tammy more than a passing thought, he couldn't allow himself to get involved with anyone in Buckshot Hills. His plan was to fly back to Phila-delphia as soon as Stan Reynolds returned to his practice. So there was no point in considering any kind of temporary fling with the locals.

But damn. He couldn't take his eyes off little Tammy Byrd, who didn't seem so little anymore—in spite of her short stature. She couldn't be much taller than five foot one. Still, Mother Nature had packed a whole lot of woman in her.

He couldn't seem to do anything but gawk at her and stumble along in his thoughts. Of course, it was just the metamorphosis that had him amazed. Wasn't it?

As one second stretched into another, she finally broke the silence with a nervous chuckle.

"What's the matter, Doc? Cat got your tongue?"

Mike, who'd been scanning the length of her again, stopped long enough to look into her eyes—those dazzling blue eyes with lush dark lashes. He'd expected to see a spark of feminine pride in them, as well as the hint of a confident grin splashed on her face. But her expression revealed a bit of apprehension.

Hadn't she realized that the new Tammy had knocked him completely off stride and that he was the one who ought to be uneasy?

Maybe not.

Okay, then. If she hadn't figured it out, he certainly wasn't going to spell it out for her.

So he tossed her a smile and said, "You ought to wear dresses more often."

Tammy ran her hands along the sleek fabric that clung to her hips. She was treading uncharted waters here.

She'd never had a man look at her with such intensity before. And while it was a little nerve wracking since she had no idea what to say or where to go from here, it also felt good.

Amazingly good.

A sense of sexual power surged through her, and for the first time ever, she was glad to be a girl—or rather, make that a woman.

She might be way off base, but it seemed as if things had suddenly changed between them. Was Doc at a loss, just like she was? And was he eager to spend a little time with her, too?

If so, the makeover had worked even better than she'd hoped. Yet as nice as the two-way attraction was, she realized he'd soon tell her that he had to go, but for some reason, he continued to stand there, gazing at her and setting her heart and her hormones pumping.

Something swirled around them, something so strong and real, she could almost cut it with a pock-etknife—which she didn't have on her right now. Not that she'd do anything to put a stop to it. The heat in Doc's gaze was enough to make her want to fan herself.

She probably ought to say or do something, but before she could come up with an actual game plan, she spoke without thinking it through. "Would you like to take a walk?"

The minute the invitation rolled out her mouth, her cheeks warmed to the bone. What must he think of her?

If she could have reeled in the words, she would have done it in a heartbeat. As it was, she had to wait for him to tell her he was way too busy for leisurely strolls. And that she was silly to even suggest it.

Doc glanced down at her feet, at the heels she wore.

Well, duh. She clearly wasn't dressed for that sort of thing.

"I can change," she said.

His gaze lifted. "Please don't."

A beat of silence followed, then his expression softened. "I'm sorry. I knew you weren't suggesting a hike or a full-on tour of the ranch."

Well, in a way, that's exactly what she'd had on her mind. She'd wanted to spend more time with him— away from the house. In fact, she always related with the males species when they were outdoors, where she could prove herself. But being with Doc was a whole new ball game—one she wasn't sure she could win.

"Did you want to talk privately?" he asked.

Actually, she wanted to get him alone—period. But she couldn't very well be that honest with him, that vulnerable, so she nodded and said, "I didn't make that very clear, did I? I have a question I want to ask, and I thought it would be best if we stepped outside."

Uh-oh. That was an even worse suggestion. Once they left the house, he'd be closer to his pickup—and closer to leaving altogether.

"Of course," he said. "Let's go." He made his way to the door and then opened it for her. "After you."

Tammy couldn't recall a man ever showing her such mannerly respect, which was cool. Who would have thought that being ladylike would be…so amazing?

"Is there a reason you're all dressed up?" Doc asked, as they crossed the porch.

"Jenna and I went shopping today, and we just got back."

Okay, so she'd avoided answering his question, while

making a truthful comment—a trick she'd used on her dad once or twice. But she couldn't very well admit that she'd gone to extremes to knock his socks off.

As Tammy stepped off the porch and into the yard, her ankles wobbled. She gasped and swayed on her feet.

Doc reached out and grabbed her, holding her steady.

Holding *her*.

His left hand gripped her forearm, while the other slipped around her waist. His touch, his concerned gaze, his musky, mountain-fresh scent, nearly turned her inside out.

Her hormones were running amok, and her heart was pounding like a son of a gun. She could blame some of her escalated pulse rate on the near mishap, but not all of it. Being held in Doc's arms so tenderly, so... Well, all she really knew was that everything feminine inside had gone completely haywire.

Or was that a normal reaction?

If she had more experience with this sort of thing, she might know for sure.

"Are you okay?" Doc asked.

She couldn't very well admit that she'd never worn high heels before and that a mama duck could have done a better job keeping her balance in those fool things. So she said, "I twisted my ankle."

"Can you walk on it?"

In her bare feet, she could. And while she might be a little backward when it came to showing her womanly side, she wasn't a fool. All she needed to do was trip up and cause her makeover plan to blow up in her face.

"Yes," she said, "I can walk, but I'm going to take off

these new shoes. They're a little too big to begin with, and I think there's something wrong with one of them."

She slipped off the heels, promising herself she'd practice walking in them when she was alone. Then she picked them up and placed them on the porch.

"So what did you want to talk to me about?" he asked.

She wouldn't be so bold as to ask him out on a date. Wasn't the guy supposed to do the asking?

Either way, she had to come up with a question of some kind for him. Something that had nothing to do with him or her. And the first one to come to mind was something she'd been thinking about ever since he'd told her that Tex only had a few weeks left to live.

"I'd asked before how long you thought my grandfather had left. But I was wondering. Will he suffer? And will he have to be in a hospital at the end?"

"I'm prescribing pain medication now, so I hope to keep his discomfort at a minimum," Doc said. "And as for the hospital, he'd like to die at home. So I'm going to do everything I can to keep him here."

She nodded, trying to wrap her mind around it all— the suffering, the impending death, the loss.

"I'm sorry. I wish I had better news."

She glanced down at her bare feet, pondering her response before meeting Doc's gaze. When their eyes met, she said, "I hardly know the man, and while that might seem like it will make his passing easier on me, it really doesn't. I can't help grieving for the wasted years when I could have had a relationship with him. And now that we've met, I'm going to lose him for good in a matter of weeks. And that's not enough time to even scratch the surface of who Tex Byrd really is."

As tears welled in her eyes, Doc lifted the arm he'd wrapped around her waist and placed his hand on her shoulder. "I'm sorry you have to go through this."

"Me, too."

His gentle touch and the compassion in his gaze offered a comfort she hadn't expected, an intimacy she'd been longing for ever since the day she first saw him.

Wouldn't it be nice if they became close enough that he could offer her a hug instead?

Either way, she'd take what he was giving her now, savoring the way his fingers warmed her from the inside out, the way his eyes locked on hers.

Still, there was another question that churned inside of her and begged to come out, one that had nothing to do with her grandfather. So as his hand trailed over her upper arm until he removed it altogether, she asked, "Would you like to stay for dinner?"

"Thanks. In all honesty, a home-cooked meal sounds good, especially since I've been eating out a lot, but I'd better take a rain check this time. You have a lot of family here, and I don't want to be an imposition."

Doc could never be an imposition. Not to Tammy, anyway.

Besides, with the family rift in full swing and a little gray cloud of awkwardness hovering over the ranch, everyone tended to eat alone. And she'd love to have some company for a change, especially his.

"It's really no trouble," she said.

"I appreciate the offer, Tammy. Maybe next time."

He was probably just being polite, but Tammy couldn't

help wondering what he would have said if she'd invited him to eat with her alone—a private meal, where none of the others would chance upon them.

Maybe he'd have been more inclined to agree. Goodness, a girl could dream, couldn't she?

And if truth be told, Tammy would much rather have the kitchen to herself. She could even give Barbara a night off. And she'd whip up the tastiest meal she could think of....

As her thoughts drifted to the cookbooks she'd found in the nightstand in the dream cabin, particularly *Romantic Dinners for Two,* an idea struck. Tammy was a whiz when it came to cooking and baking, even if she did say so herself.

And didn't they always say that the way to a man's heart was through his stomach?

Savannah had probably figured that out, which was why those cookbooks were in the cabin. She'd probably hosted a romantic evening or two there, too.

Oh, wow. Maybe Tammy could do the same thing.

Of course, she'd have to ask Tex if she could officially remove the padlock on the dream cabin. It was one thing to break in through the back window and snoop around. But it was something else to completely make herself at home without an actual invitation.

"Well, I'd better head back to town," Doc said.

As much as Tammy wanted to keep him here, she couldn't come up with another excuse to prolong his stay.

But that didn't mean she wouldn't spring the dinner question on him again—once she'd secured a romantic place for just the two of them.

Tammy tossed him a genuine smile. "I'll see you tomorrow."

"You bet." Then he strode toward his pickup.

He was about to drive off into the sunset, leaving her in the dust, but Tammy couldn't be happier.

She had a game plan. And if everything worked out the way she wanted it to, she and Doc would have that romantic dinner if it was the last thing she did.

On the drive back to town, Mike tried to focus on the road ahead, but his thoughts remained on Tammy Byrd. He'd never imagined how womanly she would look under that flannel and denim.

Well, that's not entirely true. When she came into the clinic with that shoulder injury, he'd gotten a pretty good idea of what she'd been hiding. And his thoughts had taken off in a sexual direction.

But today, after seeing her dolled up and in a sexy dress, he'd been completely floored. Who would have guessed that with a little makeup, a change of hairstyle and a black, slinky dress, the cowgirl would morph into a knockout?

And that he would be dazzled by her—so much so, that he'd nearly agreed to tour the ranch and stay for dinner.

Tammy had turned out to be prettier than he'd ever imagined. There was also something about her he found unpredictable and intriguing. And her innocence was refreshing.

She wasn't anything like the women he'd known in Philadelphia, especially Katrina, who'd gone out of her way to woo him when they'd first met.

Of course, it hadn't taken long to convince him to ask her out. She was a beautiful blonde and had a great personality. He'd also come to find out that she'd had a selfish side, although recently she'd been doing her best to convince him otherwise.

She'd called him again last night, and that time he hadn't given her any excuses about needing to hang up.

"I'm sorry about the way things ended between us," she'd told him. "I made a big mistake, Mike. And I want to make it up to you."

He hadn't been sure how she planned to do that— or if he even wanted her to, so he'd merely said, "I accept your apology."

"I can come out to Texas and we can talk more," she'd said.

"You don't need to do that. Let's give it some time."

"I think we've let enough time pass already."

While he was willing to forgive and forget, he was leery of falling back into a relationship with a woman who might not be a team player, even though she insisted she would be from here on out.

Surprisingly, Tammy flashed across his mind, and he envisioned that sprinkle of freckles across her nose, those amazing blue eyes filled with spunk, those womanly curves that made a man wish he had a right to reach for her whether she stumbled or not.

Why did he find Tammy so intriguing, especially now?

Sure, the makeover had nearly taken the breath right out of him. But maybe it was because she was so different from Katrina.

Either way, there was no way he'd get involved with

anyone in Buckshot Hills. His future was in Philly, where he was eager to return and start up his medical practice.

A lot rode on his success—his mom's retirement, for one thing. She'd worked her fingers to the bone to provide a home for him. When Mike had been a kid, there hadn't been money for many extras, and that was something he was determined to change.

Growing up, he'd seen the estate and the luxurious lifestyle his mother's boss had, and a medical degree allowed him to provide a world like that for his mom that had once been forbidden to her.

She was one of the most selfless women he'd ever met. And she deserved to live a life of comfort and leisure now that she was reaching retirement age.

For a man who'd once thought he had life mapped out for himself, Mike had landed in a brand-new world—and one he was determined to escape as soon as his old debt was paid.

Once Stanley Reynolds had finished his treatment and came back to Buckshot Hills and to his medical practice, Mike could return to Philadelphia. There he would work long hours and do whatever it took to build a practice of his own. He might be getting a slow start, but he'd make up for lost time. And that meant romance and dating would have to wait.

When the day came that he did get involved with another woman—be it Katrina or someone he'd yet to meet—he'd want to be sure that she didn't have a selfish streak or ulterior motives.

He'd been fooled once, but he couldn't afford to let it happen again.

Chapter Seven

Tammy stood at her grandfather's bedside, noting the old man's wan coloring, the gaunt cheeks, the frail movements. He was clearly weaker than he'd been when she'd talked to him the first time. He even seemed to have declined since their last chat.

They talked for a while about the weather, about the cost of alfalfa. He shared a couple of anecdotes about growing up on his daddy's ranch, how he'd loved Texas history—enough to name both his sons after heroes William Travis and Sam Houston.

As she listened to his stories, she realized that she actually liked the old man, and not just because he was related to her. They shared a love of the land and cattle.

She hoped Tex had come to the same conclusion about her, that they'd drawn close. Well, as close as the circumstances—a terminal illness and a crazy family feud—would allow.

Either way, it was time to lay her request on the table, especially since doing so would also provide her with an opening to ask the questions she'd been harboring since hearing Savannah's name.

"I found a cabin on the ranch that had the windows boarded up," she said. "And I wondered if it would be all right with you if I aired it out—and maybe even cleaned it up."

Tex didn't respond for the longest time. Then he let out a weary sigh. "I suppose it's time to do that. After next weekend, we'll be unlocking a lot of old memories—the good and the bad."

"You mean bad memories about Savannah?" Tammy asked.

Tex grimaced.

Tammy couldn't tell whether it was from the mention of the woman's name or from physical pain.

When she feared he wasn't going to say anything at all, he clicked his tongue. "Thirty-some-odd years is a long time to hold a grudge, don't you think?"

She nodded. "Yes, I do." And she couldn't help wondering if those rumors she'd heard were true. "Did Savannah cause the family rift?"

"I'm not going to get into that now. I took sides once, but I won't do it again. Your father and your uncle will have to hash things out when Sunday rolls around, although I hope they've done that already."

"Sam isn't here yet," Tammy said. "And when my dad first arrived at The Flying B, I asked him about the falling-out they'd had. He mentioned that his brother had done something unforgivable, then he clammed up."

"That's how it's been between them since the day

things blew up. And how's that working for them? I'll tell you right now—" Tex coughed and sputtered. Then he took a moment to catch his breath before he continued. "It hasn't worked out very well for me. I missed out on being a part of my grandchildren's lives."

And now he was trying to make things right, even though he was dying.

"So go ahead and take the damn lock off that door," Tex said. "It's time we all began a healing process."

As the old man closed his eyes, his head settled back onto the pillow.

Tammy wouldn't quiz him anymore. He clearly didn't want to discuss it with her. Besides, Sunday was just around the corner. And when the day of reckoning finally dawned, the secrets would all pour out, and she'd finally have the answers she wanted.

Still, she stood there a moment longer. Then she reached down and placed her hand on top of his. "Get some rest. I'll be back to see you later," she told her grandfather. Then she stepped into the hall and headed for the mudroom.

She wanted to get that cabin ready for company— possibly tomorrow night—so she would need a few things.

After filling a bucket with cleaning supplies, Tammy gathered a broom, mop and clean rags. Then she headed to the dream cabin.

If Doc was coming for dinner, she wouldn't have to risk sharing him with the rest of her family—even though they all seemed to be keeping to themselves and rarely ate together.

She'd also have to drive to town for the groceries she

would need, as well as some candles and wine. She had big plans for tomorrow night.

And big plans for Doc. The man might not put much stock in the fact that Tammy could rope and ride like Annie Oakley. But would it help if he learned that she could also cook like Betty Crocker?

Well, she could. And she didn't need a tutor, either. Her dad even boasted about her skill in the kitchen.

More than once, her father had told his friends, "My Tammy can throw an old boot in a pot of boiling water and, with a few herbs and spices, make it taste like homemade beef stew."

While Tammy had been known to complain at times about having to be the chief cook and bottle washer at home, the truth was, she actually enjoyed trying new recipes and preparing meals. But she'd never admit it in a million years. Otherwise, she might have been forced off the ranch and into the kitchen for good.

On her way to the cabin, she stopped by the barn and picked up a pair of bolt cutters. There was no reason to risk falling out of the window again. She was going to need two good arms if she wanted to whip up a special meal and spend a quiet—and hopefully romantic—evening with Doc.

Ten minutes later, she'd removed the old padlock and entered the cabin. She opened the front window to let in some fresh air. Then she got to work in the kitchen. While she scrubbed the counters and the stove, she realized that the place wasn't as neglected as she'd thought—no mold or rotting wood. For the most part, it was only musty and covered with dust. Savannah, the last one to stay here, had left things clean.

Someone had unplugged the fridge, leaving it open a crack. So after wiping it down, Tammy found the cord and plugged it into the socket. Now all she had to do was fill it with food and plan a special dinner for two.

She entered the bathroom, with its old faucets and pale blue tile. Since Savannah had clearly left the place clean and tidy, the only thing Tammy had to do, besides mopping the floor and scouring the sink, was to deal with the water marks in the toilet. A quick flush helped a little. She didn't have a scrub brush with her, but she poured a good bit of bleach into the bowl, then let it sit.

By the time Tammy had finally cleaned and freshened up the cabin, the sun had slipped low in the western sky. But instead of returning to the ranch house, she went into the small bedroom.

She'd already stripped the mattress, planning to wash the linens, as well as the chenille spread, tonight. Then she would replace them tomorrow. She'd also dusted the bureau and wound up the old alarm clock that had stopped thirty-some years ago.

But there was something else she needed to do, something she wanted to take with her—the cookbooks.

So she opened the top drawer of the nightstand and pulled them out. Yet instead of leaving with them, she turned on the lamplight, took a seat on the edge of the mattress and opened the one she was most curious about, *Romantic Dinners for Two*.

As she scanned the pages, stopping to look at the colorful photos, she lay back on the pillow, settling into the softness. The last thing she'd planned to do was to doze off, but after exerting so much elbow grease over the past few hours, she couldn't help closing her eyes for just a minute. But one minute turned into another, and before she knew it, she drifted off to sleep.

The small alarm clock tick-tocked on the bureau, but Tammy no longer heard it. Instead, she slipped into another world, where the sights and sounds were all outdoors.

She stood in the doorway of the cabin and studied the full moon that cast a gossamer glow over the ranch. An amorous cricket called to its mate, and in the distance, a horse whinnied.

Her feet bare, she padded across the plank flooring and made her way to the chipped wood railing. In the cool evening breeze, she caught a whiff of night blooming jasmine. She closed her eyes to savor the sounds and scents of the ranch at night.

"There you are," a man said softly.

Tammy opened her eyes to see Doc approaching the porch, where she stood. He was wearing dark slacks, a light green shirt and a dazzling smile that turned her heart inside out.

"Everything looks great," he said, pointing behind her. "Thanks for going to all this trouble for me."

Tammy glanced over her shoulder at the small linen-draped table set for two and adorned with a red rose in a bud vase, a flickering candle and an open bottle of wine.

Oh, yes. Of course. She'd invited Doc to have dinner with her at the cabin.

"It was no trouble," she said.

Doc climbed the steps and made his way to the table. When he pulled out a chair for her, she took a seat. Then he sat across from her.

She hadn't noticed before, but from inside the cabin, music played soft and slow.

Somewhere in the night, a phone rang. She tried to ignore the annoying jingle, but it grew into a shrill.

She turned to Doc, who'd heard it, too.

She blinked several times, then opened her eyes, only to find herself staring at the bedroom ceiling—and her cell phone ringing.

Rather than wonder who was calling, she rued the annoyance that had wakened her and ended her dream.

Disappointment crept into her voice as she answered the call. "Hello?"

"Hi, sweetie," Barbara said. "Dinner's been ready for a while. Where are you? Should I keep your plate warm?"

Tammy blinked again, trying to shake off the effects of her nap while still holding tight to the awesome dream of Doc staring across the table at her, a buzz of sexual awareness swirling around them so intense she could practically touch it.

She'd never had a dream so vivid, so real.

"Are you there?" Barbara asked. "Do we have a bad connection?"

Uh-oh. Tammy sat up, swung her feet over the feather mattress and stood. "I'm sorry, Barbara. I'll be there in a few minutes." She just had to clear her head and gather her cleaning supplies.

As she hit End to disconnect the call, she couldn't help thinking about that amazing dream. Before heading for the door, she scanned the small bedroom one last time, her eyes lighting on the feather bed on which she'd slept.

Her breath caught as she remembered the legend surrounding the bed—and the belief that the dreams a person had while sleeping in that bed came true.

She wasn't superstitious by nature. Nor was she one to believe in magic. But come hell or high water, she would do whatever it took to make that dream come true.

First thing tomorrow morning, she was going to drive to the nearest grocery store. Then she'd create a chicken risotto dish, as well as a salad with her home-made vinaigrette dressing. Dessert would be Texas chocolate cake, which she knew for a fact would impress anyone.

She had the recipe memorized right down to the fudge frosting. Of course, she'd have to borrow a cake pan from Barbara, as well as measuring spoons and a sifter. But everything else she would need was already in the cabin.

After the prep work, she'd wait for Doc to arrive for his daily exam of Tex. When he was done, she'd invite him to stay for dinner—in the privacy of the dream cabin.

All she had to do now was to re-create everything she'd envisioned just moments ago. The table setting on the small porch would be easy. She'd have to buy red roses, a candle and wine. That shouldn't be a problem.

Then she would wait for Doc to arrive—and agree to eat with her. The opportunity of a lifetime was hers—if she didn't screw it up.

As she left the cabin, her mind was abuzz with romantic possibilities—until she realized she might be wrong about Doc truly wanting a rain check on dinner until he could be alone with her.

If she'd misunderstood, if she'd read him wrong and he declined, she'd…

Well, she'd offer the chicken risotto to Hugh and some of the ranch hands. Then she'd create a brand-new meal the next day and invite Doc all over again. Eventually, he'd have to agree. Wouldn't he?

If there was anything at all to that dream legend, he certainly would. And Tammy, who ought to be skeptical of the claim, chose to believe it was true. Because if she wanted Doc, she was going to need all the magic she could get.

Mike hoped he hadn't made a mistake by agreeing to have dinner with Tammy at the Flying B tonight, but for the past couple of days, after he'd finished checking in on Tex, she'd invited him to stay and eat with her in one of the cabins. And each time she had done so, she'd offered him a tempting menu.

Truth be told, he'd nearly agreed the very first time she'd asked him…and not just because chicken risotto had sounded good. He actually found himself looking forward to running into her lately.

Ever since she'd gone shopping with her cousin Jenna and met him at the door wearing that sexy black dress, he'd been… Well, he'd really sat up and taken notice of her. He'd also been tempted to start something that he wouldn't be in Texas long enough to see through. And with her grandfather dying, it didn't seem right to suggest a…what? A temporary friendship with benefits?

Yet for some reason, when she asked him to stay for dinner again, he'd agreed, reminding himself that it was Saturday, the weekend was in full swing and he'd gotten sick and tired of spending all his free time at home in front of the TV.

That was true, of course, but there'd been something else going on.

When he'd first arrived at the Flying B this afternoon and parked in his usual spot, Tammy had been perched on the top railing on a nearby corral, almost as if she'd been waiting for him. Then again, he could never be sure about anything with her.

He'd remained in the car for a beat, intrigued by her. And wondering what she was doing, seated on that railing while wearing a blue sundress that really set off the color of her eyes. She'd been barefoot, too, with toes polished a pretty shade of pink. And when she'd glanced his way and smiled, she'd reminded him of a fairy—or maybe even a wood nymph.

For a moment, he'd been mesmerized. In fact, he'd damn near forgotten why he'd driven out to the Flying B in the first place.

"Hey, there," she'd said, as she climbed from the railing, her movements girlish and more in line with those of the cowgirl he'd first met. But when a breeze kicked up the hem of her dress, revealing a shapely leg, he'd found himself moonstruck once again. And a bit speechless.

What did a man say to a woman like her?

He'd be damned if he knew. Still, he opened the driver's door and got out of his truck.

"How about dinner tonight?" she'd asked, as she approached him.

She'd mentioned pot roast yesterday, and he'd made an excuse on why he had to pass then. But he'd gone home and fixed a sandwich instead, then kicked himself for missing out on a homemade meal. Who would have thought the cowgirl he'd first met could cook?

"I'm making carne asada," she added.

He loved Mexican food and wondered if she'd known how tempted he was.

Okay, so the temptation went beyond the food.

"Are you hungry?" she asked.

He certainly was. Just standing here, looking at her, at the sparkle in those pretty blue eyes, stirred his hunger in other ways. And before he could give it another thought, his resolve bit the dust. "As a matter of fact, I am. And dinner sounds good."

At that, she'd flashed him a hundred-watt smile. "Great. It'll be ready whenever you are."

Then she'd given him directions to the cabin where she'd prepared the meal.

He'd stuck around outside for a while, just talking to her…and not about anything in particular. There was just something about Tammy that fascinated him more each time he saw her.

It was funny how he hadn't really noticed her at first. But now? For some damn reason, he found himself thinking about her at the strangest times—even when he wasn't on her grandfather's ranch.

So now here he was, about to have dinner with her. And actually looking forward to it. After leaving Tex's bedroom, he gave a few instructions to Tina, the housekeeper. Then he made his way outdoors and followed the path to the knoll Tammy had pointed out to him earlier.

The sun had already begun to set, streaking the horizon in shades of pink and gray. There was something peaceful about the ranch even a city boy found appealing.

The soles of his loafers crunched on the dirt path. When he spotted the cabin, his stomach actually growled.

Tammy had said she'd have dinner ready when he arrived. He hoped so. He'd had a light lunch today and was ready for something hearty.

As he reached the cabin, he spotted a table had been set up on the porch. A red rose sat in a bud vase next to a flickering candle. He wasn't sure what he'd been expecting, but certainly not this.

A smile stole across his face. He'd never met a woman like Tammy before, and something told him he never would again. He might even miss her when he returned to Philadelphia.

"Hey," Tammy said, as she walked out the front door wearing the slinky black dress that hugged her curves and made it difficult for him to focus on anything other than her.

"Thanks for coming," she said. "Can I get you something to drink? Lemonade, an ice-cold beer…? Maybe a glass of red wine?"

"What are you having?" he asked.

"Wine. I just uncorked a bottle."

"Sounds good to me." He scanned the romantic table setting. "So what's all of this about?"

"I thought…" Tammy paused and bit down on her lower lip. "Well, I thought you might like a little more atmosphere than the inside of a small, cramped cabin."

Okay. He supposed that made sense. "But what about dinner? Tex has a cook—and a good one at that. So it seems weird that you'd be skipping her meals and preparing your own."

"Barbara is pretty territorial in the kitchen. And since I love to cook, I started coming out here to do my own thing."

"You eat alone?"

"Not if I don't have to. That's why I invited you." She tossed him a breezy smile, her eyes sparkling as though she'd had some plan he wasn't privy to.

But then again, who knew what Tammy had on her mind?

"Will you excuse me for a minute?" she asked.

"Sure."

She slipped into the house and returned with an uncorked bottle of merlot and two goblets. "If you'll pour the wine, I'll bring out the food."

"Of course." Mike took the glasses from her, then filled them halfway.

Minutes later, Tammy brought out a tray with all the fixings for their meal—guacamole, salsa fresca, sour cream and cilantro. She also had a basket of warm corn tortillas.

"Just one more trip to the kitchen," she said.

Upon her return, she carried a bowl filled with seasoned pork, the aroma making his mouth water with hunger.

"This looks amazing," he said.

"I hope you like it."

"I'm sure I will." He pulled out a chair for her, and after she took a seat, he joined her.

As they filled their plates, he caught the sound of music playing softly in the background. Again, he wondered if she'd planned a romantic evening, but then let it go.

Instead, he dug in to his meal.

"You're a great cook," he said. "You ought to open a restaurant."

She brightened and leaned forward. "You think so?"

"You bet I do. In fact, I used to believe my mother was the best Mexican cook ever, but I'm going to have to tell her she's got some stiff competition."

Tammy's heart soared at the compliment. It seemed to be working, the meal, the romantic aura. Even the sunset seemed to be playing along.

She considered mentioning something about it, just in case he hadn't noticed. But she figured it was best if she let nature take its course. So she picked up her fork, speared a piece of the seasoned meat and took a bite.

When they'd both finished eating, she asked, "Are you ready for dessert?"

"I'm stuffed and probably ought to pass, but if it's as good as the carne asada, I'll make room."

Tammy smiled, then excused herself. When she returned with the flan she'd whipped up, Doc's smile lit his face. "You're going to spoil me, Tammy."

That had been the plan all along. Doc had not only noticed her, but he also appreciated her, too. Could the future look any brighter than it did right now?

After he finished the dessert, he asked if he could help her with the dishes.

"No need," she said. "I've got it all under control."

At least, she had the kitchen stuff taken care of. The romantic goodbyes—if things went the way she hoped—were another thing.

Would he kiss her? Would he ask her out on a date—a real one?

The dream she'd had while sleeping in the feather bed had only been about a meal on the cabin porch. From here on out, Tammy was on her own.

"Well, then I'd better get going," Doc said. "Thanks for dinner, Tammy. I'm glad you asked me."

And she was glad he'd accepted. Too bad they had to call it a night.

"I'll walk you to your pickup," she said.

"All right."

As they stepped down from the porch, Doc said, "Aren't you going to put on your shoes?"

She paused a moment, her bare feet resting on the soft dirt. She'd gotten dressed in the cabin. And she'd brought the black heels more for effect than anything.

Dang. She wished she felt more confident walking in the fool things. She'd been practicing, of course, and she'd gotten better. But she wasn't so sure how she'd do on a darkened dirt path.

"I'm not much of a wine drinker," she admitted, offering him a smile, "so one glass made me feel so warm and cozy that I forgot I'd slipped off my shoes earlier."

A part of that was true. The wine had given her a nice buzz. But thanks to the spell Doc cast on her whenever he was around, she'd felt that way before she'd had a single sip of merlot.

He waited while she returned to the cabin and put on the heels, then they walked together, following the pathway to the main house. Their steps were lit by a full moon, as well as the lighting on the outbuildings.

"I'm going to be making stuffed pork chops tomorrow," Tammy said, "so I hope you'll stick around after your visit."

"I might take you up on that, but maybe we should play dinner by ear."

She wasn't sure why, but she nodded.

"Tex told me your uncle and your brothers are expected to arrive on Sunday, so he scheduled that family meeting at three."

Tammy had known it would take place on Sunday, but she hadn't known when.

"I plan to be here for the meeting," Doc added. "Not in the room, of course. But I'll be on the premises. I have a feeling the stress is going to put a strain on Tex, and I think I ought to be here—just in case he needs me."

"That's really thoughtful of you, Doc."

He slowed to a stop, then turned to face her. "Can you do me a favor?"

"Sure." She gazed into his eyes, amazed that he considered her a teammate of sorts. "What is it?"

"Would you call me Mike instead of Doc?"

As a slow smile snuck across her face, she tried to reel it in. "I didn't know it bothered you to be called Doc."

"I'm okay with it. That's what everyone in Buckshot

Hills calls me. But I have to admit, it took a little getting used to at first. My mom calls me Miguel. And my friends all call me Mike."

So she'd become his *friend*. That was certainly a step in the right direction. After all, most people in Philadelphia probably called him Dr. Sanchez. At least he hadn't asked her to be that formal.

When they reached his pickup, she feared that he would merely say goodbye, then open the driver's door and slide behind the wheel. Her heart ached at the thought of losing him so soon, before she had a chance to tell him that she…

What? That she loved him? Goodness, she hardly knew him. Yet she had no idea what she was truly feeling for him. It felt so much stronger than a girlish crush.

"Thanks again for dinner," he said. "It was delicious."

"I'm glad you enjoyed it…Mike."

He stood there for a moment, as if weighing his words carefully. And she really couldn't blame him. Her future seemed to be hanging in the balance. At least, right now, as the intensity of his gaze darn near stole the breath right out of her, it certainly felt that way.

When she thought she might die from the silence, from the temptation, from the swarm of pheromones that swirled overhead, he reached out and ran his knuckles along her cheek.

The heat of his touch tingled to the bone, and her knees nearly buckled.

"I may regret this later," he said softly.

Regret what?

Her heart pounded in anticipation, not daring to hope, to dream, to…

Just like a dream come true, he lowered his mouth to hers.

Chapter Eight

Mike hadn't meant to do much more than give Tammy a simple good-night kiss, but as his lips brushed hers, as she stepped into his embrace and slipped her arms around his neck, their lips met in an explosion of stars that would put the fireworks at a Fourth of July celebration to shame.

Who would have guessed that the seemingly innocent girl could kiss like that?

As his tongue swept inside her mouth, seeking, touching, tasting, her breath caught. He drew her closer, and she leaned into him, pressing her breasts against his chest.

A jolt of heat shot through his bloodstream, unleashing a flood of desire.

He reminded himself that the physical reaction was merely biological. He'd gone without sex for months, so it was only natural to feel such an amazing arousal with a single kiss.

So while he was sorely tempted to continue kissing her until she suggested they turn around, return to the cabin and see where all this confounding attraction would lead, a sexual relationship would only complicate their lives right now. So he drew back.

When he loosened his embrace, Tammy swayed on her feet as if she'd been every bit as caught up in the hunger and heat as he'd been. So he reached for her again, holding her steady.

At least, that's the excuse he claimed for not letting go, for taking another moment to breathe in her citrusy scent—lemon blossoms, he suspected.

A beat or two later, when he figured she'd regained her balance, he released her and took a step back.

"I'm sorry," he said. "I didn't mean to do that."

"You didn't?" Suspicion glimmered in her eyes.

"Okay. So I did. But I didn't mean to let it get so out of hand."

"Don't be sorry about kissing me." She tossed him a wistful smile. "I'm glad that you did."

Yeah, well, in a way, he was, too. But it had been flat-ass crazy and not very well planned out.

For a guy who couldn't wait to get out of Buckshot Hills—and who had no intention of striking up a brief affair with his patient's granddaughter—he'd certainly tripped up by giving Tammy a kiss better suited for lovers. She was bound to expect more from him after that.

Hell, even he wanted more at this point...no matter how complicated things might get.

They stood like that for a moment, the kiss hovering over them like a pending cloudburst.

Would a brief affair really be such a bad idea? After all, Mike was getting tired of spending his nights alone. And he still had no idea when he could even set a date for his flight home.

If Tammy's kiss meant anything, she wasn't a novice at sex. And she'd clearly been making the moves on him.

Maybe a sexual fling for the duration of his time in Texas wouldn't be so bad. After all, they were both adults.

Who would it hurt?

No one, he thought.

Yet something told him that might not be true. That Tammy might not fare as well with a breakup as he would. And he didn't want to hurt her. She'd become too...special, he supposed. So he took the high road.

"I'd better go," he said.

"Okay. I'll see you tomorrow." Again she smiled. And this time he noted a glimpse of innocence, of... virginity?

Or was that an act?

Who was this woman? A virgin tomboy or a skilled lover stringing him along with feigned innocence?

He'd be damned if he knew.

Either way, she belonged on a ranch—either in Buckshot Hills or elsewhere. And Mike belonged back East, in Philadelphia, at a top-notch hospital.

"Don't forget about the pork chops," she said, smiling. "And lemon meringue pie for dessert."

"Let's see what tomorrow brings," he said, not wanting to commit to anything while memories of that arousing kiss had yet to die down.

But damn. He'd always been partial to lemon meringue pie.

Not to mention a newfound fondness for the scent of lemon blossoms on soft, silky skin....

As Tammy stood in the yard and watched Doc—or rather, Mike—climb into his pickup, her lips still tingled from that soul-stirring good-night kiss they'd shared.

Never in her wildest dreams had she imagined kissing Mike would be like that, feel like that, taste like that....

As he'd gazed in her eyes, the night air had sparked with anticipation. She'd sensed it coming, and the strangest thing had happened. Any insecurity she might have had earlier disappeared in the moonlight. And her hormones and instincts had suddenly kicked into gear.

Her arms had lifted of their own accord, and she'd slipped them around his neck. If she hadn't leaned into him, she might have collapsed into a heap on the ground.

She'd feared she'd never get enough of him, and she hadn't. Much to her regret, the kiss had ended long before she was ready.

Mike had thanked her for dinner and said goodbye. Then, without a single comment about the star-spinning kiss they'd shared, he'd climbed behind the wheel of his pickup and turned on the ignition.

Now, as she watched his taillights disappear down the darkened drive, she took a deep breath, then returned to the cabin, where she went through the motions of cleaning up.

When she had everything spic and span, she decided against returning to the ranch house. Instead, she slipped out of her dress and hung it in the closet. Then, wearing only her undies, she climbed into the feather bed, with its fresh linen, and settled onto the soft mattress, willing another nocturnal vision to come her way.

Yet even though she'd fallen asleep while reliving the evening, basking in the memory of Mike's disarming smile, the spark in his caramel-hued eyes, the taste of his mouth, heat of his touch, the sandman hadn't cooperated.

The next morning, after a dreamless night, she awoke feeling refreshed, yet disappointed.

Had she already tapped the last bit of magic out of the feather bed? Was there a one-dream limit per person?

She had no idea, but she wouldn't let the possibility mar her plans for the day. She had another dinner to plan, another romantic evening to create. She also had a family meeting to look forward to. Sunday had dawned, and her uncle and her brothers would be arriving soon.

Since she didn't have time to waste daydreaming, she threw back the coverlet and got to her feet. After making the bed, she slipped into her dress, picked up her high heels and headed for the house in her bare feet.

She'd no more than entered the yard when a white, late-model Cadillac drove up and parked. She watched a middle-age man climb out. She didn't have to ask who he was. He looked enough like her father to be his brother.

And clearly, that's just who he was: Sam Houston Byrd.

"Hi there," Tammy said. "I assume you're my uncle."

Sam waited a beat before answering. "If you're right, then you must be William's daughter."

She offered him a warm, let's-put-the-past-behind-us smile and reached out for a handshake. "Tamara Kay Byrd. But everyone calls me Tammy."

He accepted her hand with a firm grip, but didn't return her smile. "Is your dad here yet?"

Before she could nod or respond, footsteps sounded at the side of the house. She turned to see her father walking into the yard, carrying a coffee mug. The moment he laid eyes on his brother, he stopped dead in his tracks. His stance stiffened.

The air grew so thick with silent emotion—anger, distrust, resentment?—that it nearly stole the breath right out of Tammy. Yet neither man spoke to the other.

As she struggled to make sense of it all—and to think of something to say to lighten things up—Sam headed toward the house. When he'd gone inside, her father scanned the length of her, taking in the dress she wore and the high heels she held in one hand.

Tammy had never gone to any of her high school proms, so she'd never even had an opportunity to come home late. But she suspected the look her dad was giving her now was pretty close to what she would have gotten if she'd snuck into the house as a teenager and found him waiting for her in the wee hours of the morning.

"Where've you been?" he asked.

"I slept in the cabin last night."

"Why?"

"I...just dozed off."

Again he scanned her length, from her bed-head hair to her bare feet and back up again. His brow furrowed as if she were sixteen and the clock had just chimed 4:00 a.m.

Goodness. Did he think she'd had a romantic encounter in the cabin?

Well, she had...sort of. But not the kind he was probably imagining...nor the kind she hoped to have with Mike someday soon.

He crossed his arms and cocked his head. "You weren't meeting up with one of the ranch hands, were you?"

One of the hands? Absolutely not. And while she'd always been a daddy's girl, had always shared a closeness, she didn't think she owed him an explanation. "I'm not a little girl anymore, Dad."

"I can see that." He gave her a paternal once-over, softening it seemed. "I had no idea just how much until I watched a metamorphosis occur on the Flying Byrd."

"I have my cousins to thank for that."

He paused a beat, as if realizing all Tammy had missed while growing up, all she'd missed because of the family feud. Then he said, "I'm glad you girls have hit it off."

Was he really? Even though they were Sam's daughters?

"I'm glad, too. Jenna and Donna are really sweet." And they'd accepted her as one of them—women, not just Byrds. "I hope you'll take time to get to know them."

He didn't respond, and as she turned toward the house, he stopped her. "You said you slept in one of the cabins last night. Which one?"

"Savannah's. The one with the feather bed."

She wasn't sure what she'd expected him to say when she'd thrown out Savannah's name. And for a moment, she thought the tall, broad-shouldered rancher she'd always looked up to might crack and crumble.

Then he rallied. "What in the hell were you doing in there? That cabin has been locked up for years."

"I know. But Grandpa Tex said I could open it up and clean it out."

At that, he drew up and stiffened. Yet he didn't respond.

"Is there some reason you wish that cabin would have stayed locked?" she asked.

He blew out a sigh, and his stance shifted. "No. Not really." Then he turned and walked back in the same direction from which he'd come.

Tammy merely watched him go.

Three o'clock, she told herself. *Just six or seven more hours.* Then she'd probably have the answers to her questions about her father, her uncle and the mysterious Savannah, who'd torn the Byrd family in two.

And surely Savannah had done just that.

Was there any other assumption for Tammy to make?

In the meantime, she would take a shower and dress for the day. Then she'd prepare another romantic dinner for Mike.

And she'd also come up with a surefire way to win his heart.

* * *

Nathan and Aidan, Tammy's brothers, arrived at the Flying B a little after the lunch hour. Tina, who must have been waiting for them, showed them to the cabin in which they'd be staying.

Tammy had been pleased to learn that they'd been assigned a place that was fairly close to the ranch house—and quite a ways from the dream cabin, where she and Mike would be eating tonight.

What a relief. The boys sometimes thought they had to take care of her, and she didn't need their help, especially when she was hoping for more than just dinner tonight.

After preparing the pork chops ahead of time and putting them in the cabin oven, she returned to her bedroom in the house, where she showered, fixed her hair and slipped on the pale yellow sundress she'd purchased while shopping with Jenna.

As the afternoon wore on, she was more than a little ready for Mike's arrival…and for that family meeting.

Apparently, so were the others, who'd begun to gather in the living room, including her brothers who'd come straight from the wilds of Montana. Before long, that same heavy, breath-stealing emotion returned, filling the air around them.

Tammy tried to make small talk with Jenna and Donna to ease the tension. But her cousins appeared to be just as uneasy about the situation as she was, so her efforts didn't seem to work.

When the clock on the mantel finally chimed three, Mike had yet to arrive. Tammy hoped he hadn't been called to an emergency.

"It's time," Tina announced from the hallway. "Tex is ready for you."

Tammy fell into line with the others, as the housekeeper led them to the old man's bedroom, where a few chairs had been set out. But she was too nervous to sit, so she made her way to where her dad and brothers stood.

As Sam and his daughters took the opposite side of Tex's bed, Tammy realized that Tex might be dying, but the division between the families was still alive and kicking.

"You all know why I called you here," Tex said, his voice even weaker than it had been a week ago, when Tammy had first met him. "My days are numbered. And there's something I need to do before I go. Something I should have done years ago."

Sam and William lowered their heads, as if meeting the old man's gaze was tough.

"There'll be a reading of the will after I'm gone," Tex said. "And at that time, I won't be around to tell you why I've divided things up the way I did."

Tammy glanced across the room at her cousins, Jenna and Donna. She wondered what they were thinking, what they were feeling.

Were they, like her, at the ranch because it was the right thing to do, and not because they expected anything in return?

If truth be told, Tammy wouldn't have blamed the old man if he'd excluded them all from his will.

After a moment, Tex spoke again. "I'm leaving the east half of the Flying B, including the house, barns, cabins and outbuildings, to Tammy, Jenna and Donna."

The sisters glanced at each other, clearly surprised by their grandfather's gift, then looked at Tammy before turning their attention back to the old man.

"As part of the terms of the will," Tex said, "you'll have to keep the property in the family. You'll also be required to provide jobs for Tina Crandall and Barbara Eyler as long as they want to stay on the Flying B. I'm not sure about Tina's plans for the future, but Barbara intends to retire soon. However, I don't want her to leave before she's ready. Both those women have been good, loyal employees for more than thirty years. And I want them to have jobs at the Flying B for as long as they want."

Tammy looked across the room at her cousins, wondering what they'd have to say about sharing the ranch with her. Jenna, who worked with horses, might be happy about it. But Donna? She'd probably rather hightail it home to the city as fast as her little high heels would take her.

"There'll be some money for you girls, too," Tex added. "Enough to help you fix things up a bit—in the house and barns. Hugh knows all about this. And he'll be able to offer suggestions and advice. Listen to him. He knows what he's talking about."

Tammy wondered if her cousins would insist on selling the place…once Grandpa Byrd passed. She hoped not. Living in Buckshot Hills would make it a lot easier for her and Mike to build a relationship.

Tex coughed several times, then reached for a glass of water on his nightstand, his hand shaking. After he took a drink, he cleared his voice and said, "I'm giving Aidan and Nathan the undeveloped property on the west side of the ranch, along with the mineral rights. There'll be some cash for you boys, too. You can use it to mine the property—if you want to. But if anything ever comes of the drilling or mining, you'll have to share a percentage with the girls. It's all laid out in the will."

Tammy's brothers glanced first at each other, then at the old man.

"I'm also leaving something to one of my ranch hands. He's been like a son to me. And I don't have to tell you how much I valued that kind of relationship over the past few years, especially since I lost the sons I had."

Tammy stole a peek at her uncle Sam, whose head was bowed. She didn't dare turn and look at her dad, but she suspected he was feeling just as sheepish, just as…guilty?

"The rest of my money, investments and assets go to William and Sam. You might be surprised to know it's a fair sum. As much as I'd wanted to stipulate that you only get it if you end that blasted feud and bury the hatchet, I didn't do it. I just hope you'll see the wisdom in doing that on your own."

Neither of the men responded, and as that heavy silence filled the room, Tex blew out a weary sigh. "That's it. I've said my piece. Now go on out and let me nap. Dying, like parenting, is hard work."

As they all began to file out, Tammy followed behind Nathan and Aidan. She hated to leave her grandfather like that, but she knew how draining that meeting had been. She would come back to visit him later, to thank him for the inheritance and to ask if there was anything she could do to make his passing easier on him. It seemed to be the least she could do.

When the family reached the living room and began to disperse, Tammy spotted Mike seated on the sofa, and her heart soared. Had a man ever been so handsome?

He stood, and her heart skittered through her chest like a stone skipping across the surface of a pond.

Their gazes locked for one amazing, blood-stirring moment, then he reached for his medical bag and headed down the hall to check on Grandpa Byrd.

Nathan and Aidan went outdoors, as did her dad and her uncle Sam. She'd been tempted to join her father, to offer him a hug or something. But she thought the brothers might want to talk to each other. Instead, the older men went in opposite directions.

"Did that surprise you?" Jenna asked Tammy. "To learn that he's giving the ranch to us?"

Tammy nodded. "I hadn't expected anything at all, let alone the Flying B."

"I know how much this ranch means to Tex," Jenna said. "So I'm honored that he entrusted it to us."

Tammy had come to the same conclusion. She glanced at Donna, who seemed to be deep in thought. Rumor had it that her city cousin was facing some financial difficulties, although Tammy didn't know that for sure.

But if that was the case, was Donna wishing they could sell the property and split the proceeds?

Maybe. And if so, Tammy felt sorry for her. However, their grandfather had said that selling the property wasn't an option. And Tammy was happy about that. If a romance between her and Mike was going to flourish, she needed to stay in Buckshot Hills. And now she had a good reason to do so.

"I'm not a rancher," Donna said.

Jenna seemed to think on that a moment. Then she said, "What about turning it into a B and B? We could fix up the cabins and offer horseback riding for our guests."

"Are you suggesting a dude ranch?" Donna asked.

"I guess so. We might even be able to offer them a chance to ride on a cattle drive."

"Like the movie *City Slickers?*" Donna asked.

"Yes, something like that. It's something to think about."

Tammy agreed, but the only contribution she had was to head up the cattle drive Jenna had mentioned. Trouble was, Tammy wasn't so sure she wanted to go back to the cowgirl days. She'd begun to enjoy dressing like a woman—and exchanging those granny panties for silk and lace.

Jenna had been right. Just knowing she wore those sexy undies under her clothes made a huge difference in the way she felt, the way she carried herself.

"Do you guys want to go outside and talk more about it?" Jenna asked. "We could take a walk and get a better look at the property."

Tammy glanced at the doorway that led down the hall, then back to her cousin. "Can that walk wait a bit?"

"Sure," Jenna said. "We have plenty of time."

Thank goodness she'd agreed. Tammy didn't want to discuss the possibility of creating a B and B right now, no matter how intriguing the idea might be. With Mike just steps away, she had other things on her mind.

"There's a lot to think about," Donna said, "a lot to consider."

Yes, that was true. And not just about the Flying B. Tammy had more immediate concerns.

Like inviting Mike back to the cabin again tonight.

Just as Mike had suspected, the family meeting had really taxed his elderly patient.

"Your blood pressure is elevated," Mike said. "And your breathing is labored. I'm going to increase your oxygen level and give you a sedative."

Tex chuffed. "Maybe you ought to just fill that hypodermic needle with a triple dose and send me on to greener pastures."

Mike didn't respond to Tex's sarcasm. Instead, he adjusted the oxygen and then gave him the injection.

"Did the meeting go well?" he asked, as he disposed of the used needle.

"As good as could be expected. I'm just glad it's finally out of the way—and that all hell didn't break loose."

Mike suspected that the reason no one blew up was out of respect for the dying man. Patching up a thirty-five-year-old feud wouldn't be simple or easy.

Either way, he stood by Tex's bedside, waiting for the sedative to take effect.

Several minutes later, the old man closed his eyes. Mike watched his chest rise and fall, noting the labored breathing had eased.

When he was sure Tex was resting easy, he left

the bedroom, softly closed the door and headed down the hall. He found the living room empty, except for Tammy, who stood at the window, peering out into the yard.

Apparently, she was so deep in thought that she hadn't heard his approach, so he stopped in the doorway and watched her for a moment.

Her dark hair hung loose again today, the glossy strands lying soft against her back in a jumble of curls a man's hands could get lost in. The kind of curls that would look good splayed against a pillow.

He supposed he could say something to let her know he was here—or even continue into the room—but he actually enjoyed having the opportunity to study her while she was unaware of his presence.

When he'd first spotted her earlier today, when she was coming out of Tex's room after the meeting, he'd noticed her clothing—stylish black slacks and a white, feminine blouse. But he hadn't realized how nicely those pants hugged her shapely hips.

A part of him wanted her to turn and meet his gaze, while another thought it best if he slipped quietly into the kitchen and out the back door before she actually did turn around and spot him. After all, they would probably have to address the heated kiss they'd shared last night—and what they wanted to do about the sexual attraction that sizzled between them.

What made that decision a bit complicated was the fact that Mike was leaving Buckshot Hills in the near future. And he had no idea how much longer he'd be in town—whether it was weeks or months. Yet the more time he spent away from his life in Philadelphia, the less he liked thinking about remaining celibate indefinitely.

As if Tammy had finally sensed his presence, she turned. When her gaze met his, her lips parted. And his heart rate took off like a shot.

Damn, if she wasn't a sight to behold.

Shaking off the mounting desire to kiss her senseless, he crossed the room as if he'd been moving all along.

"How's Tex?" she asked.

"He's okay now. The meeting proved to be a little stressful, but I gave him some medication to help. And I stayed until he was sleeping peacefully."

"You're an amazing doctor. He's lucky to have you. In fact, we all are." Tammy's smile, along with the admiration and who knew what other expressions lighting her eyes, sent his ego soaring as though he'd just been honored by the American Medical Association.

"Thanks," he said, downplaying both her praise and his reaction to it. "I'm just doing what Doc Reynolds would have done."

He probably should tell her that Doc Reynolds would be returning soon, and that Mike would then be free to go, but for some reason, he didn't want to think about leaving town just yet.

"I have dinner in the oven," she said. "Will you stay and eat with me?"

As tempting as that was, it didn't seem like a good idea—for more reasons than the one he was going to give her.

"It's probably not a good night. Your whole family is here—whether they eat in the house or in the privacy of their rooms. And there's bound to be a lot of tension. I don't want to add to it."

She bit down on her bottom lip, as if pondering his reason. Then she nodded, as if finding it valid. "Okay. But how about tomorrow?"

He couldn't help but grin. "We'll see. Okay?"

She flashed him a pretty smile. "You bet."

He could have told her goodbye at that point and turned away. Instead, he reached out and ran his knuckles along her cheek, tempted to do so much more than that.

"What am I going to do about you?" he asked.

Her eyes sparked, and a grin tugged at her lips. "I'm sure you'll think of something."

She was right about that. And that was the problem, especially if he wanted to leave town without any emotional attachments—or regrets.

But he shook it off, determined to put some space between him and temptation. "I'll see you tomorrow— unless Tex has a setback, in which case, I'll come back sooner. Just give me a call."

"Of course."

With that, he walked out the door and headed for his pickup.

What am I going to do about you? he'd asked her moments ago.

He thought about the dilemma all the way back to town, but he still came up with the same conclusion.

He'd be damned if he knew.

Chapter Nine

When Mike left the house, Tammy followed him to his truck. Yet other than telling her goodbye, he took off without saying a word, leaving her to wonder what was going on between them.

The fact that he'd gone without giving her another kiss made her a little uneasy. She certainly hoped her very first love affair wasn't over before it even had a chance to get off the ground.

What am I going to do about you? Mike had asked, his eyes searching hers as if looking for an answer she couldn't provide.

I'm sure you'll think of something, she'd said.

She certainly hoped that he would, because other than whipping up a delicious meal, she had no other ideas on how to win his heart.

Did she dare ask Jenna for advice? Her cousin had been so helpful on that shopping trip, offering all kinds of feminine tips, that they seemed to have become friends, as well as relatives.

But should Tammy just come right out and ask if Jenna had any advice or suggestions on how to seduce a man? After all, there had to be more to it than just wine, candles and song.

Or should she just leave it all up to fate and let nature run its course?

Either way, Tammy could really use a friendly face now, and Jenna fit the bill.

Of course, she had to find her first. After a scan of the yard and the outbuildings, Tammy spotted her cousin standing at the corral that was located nearest to the house. But it was still a hike. So she crossed the yard to meet her.

"Hey," Tammy said, as she approached. "What are you doing?"

"Just visiting Daphne." Jenna stroked the roan mare's neck. "She's a sweetheart."

Jenna clearly loved horses, maybe even more than Tammy did. It seemed that the two of them might have more in common than either might have once thought.

"Did you get a chance to talk to Doc?" Jenna asked.

"A little, I suppose." Tammy leaned against the railing and blew out a wistful sigh. "He finally noticed me."

"That's good."

"Yes, and I have you to thank for that."

Jenna smiled. "I'm sure he would have eventually noticed you."

Tammy didn't know about that. As she scanned the yard, she said, "I can't believe this will be ours one day."

"Neither can I. It's quite an honor—and a responsibility."

That it was. As Tammy's gaze drifted toward the dream cabin, she spotted Hugh riding his appaloosa gelding.

"Excuse me a minute," Tammy said. "I need to get rid of some pork chops." Then she called out to the ranch foreman.

Hugh reined the horse toward the corral where the women stood. "What can I do for you?"

"I have another meal to share with you and the men," Tammy said. "Are you hungry?"

"I am if you're cooking." Hugh placed a hand on the pommel of his saddle and grinned. "When it comes to cooks, Barbara is a real humdinger. But after eating the leftovers you've been giving me, I'd have to say that you rate right up there."

"Thanks." Tammy never tired of the compliments she received from those who ate her meals. "It should be done in about forty-five minutes."

"I'll stop by the cabin and pick it up."

As Hugh urged the gelding back in the direction they'd been heading, Jenna said, "I didn't know you were a cook."

"It was the one chore at home that I really enjoyed, although I never dared let my dad and brothers know that. Otherwise, they'd have kept me housebound and chained to the stove. But at night, after everyone had turned in, I used to study my mom's cookbooks. And I'd even search for other recipes online. I have to admit, I fixed a few lousy meals in the early days. But eventually, I got the hang of it."

"Maybe," Jenna said, "if Barbara retires and we do open a B and B, you could be the cook. That is, if you like that idea."

Oh, she liked it all right. She liked everything about staying in Buckshot Hills—close enough to Mike to be a contender for his heart. And while she used to fear getting stuck with kitchen duty before, back when she had to compete with her brothers on a daily basis, that didn't matter anymore. She'd left her girlhood behind, even it if it meant boots and jeans and gymkhana ribbons rather than dolls and such.

"I'd enjoy working in the kitchen," Tammy said.

Neither girl spoke for a beat, and Tammy suspected they were both thinking about the inheritance they were getting.

So she threw her thoughts ought there. "I wonder what Tex would think about us turning the Flying B into a B and B."

Jenna chuckled. "You mean, if we called it the Flying B and B?"

"I like the sound of that," Tammy said.

"Me, too. But I'm not sure what Tex would think."

"I've had a chance to spend a little time with him," Tammy said. "And something tells me he'd appreciate our efforts to make our own mark on the ranch."

"You're probably right."

"As a side note," Tammy added, "when it comes to a B and B, I'm game if you and Donna are. Do you know how she feels about it?"

"We really haven't talked much about it yet. I think it's all so new."

That struck Tammy as a bit odd. After all, if she

had a sister, especially one like Jenna, she'd be running ideas by her all the time.

Goodness. Look at her now. She'd just met her cousins, yet when it came time to confide in someone, she'd gone to Jenna.

"Are you and your sister close?" she asked, assuming—or maybe hoping—they were.

"No, not really."

That was too bad. And kind of sad, actually.

Jenna turned her attention back to the horse. "What do you think, Daphne? Does a ride sound good to you?"

Tammy hadn't been riding since she arrived at the Flying B, which was unusual. But she supposed that was to be expected. After all, her thoughts had been so darned focused on Mike. And on romantic dinners for two and goodbye kisses that could knock a gal to her knees.

"You know," Tammy said, "I'd better go check on those pork chops and pack it up for Hugh. I'll talk to you later."

As Jenna opened the corral gate, Tammy headed for the path that led to the dream cabin. She'd barely reached the knoll when she ran into her brother Aidan.

"Hey, Tam." His steps slowed. "What are you up to? Checking out your soon-to-be inheritance?"

"No, I'm going to the dream cabin."

He cocked his head, and she realized he hadn't been privy to the facts or the rumors she'd heard. So she shared what she'd learned so far about the reason for the family feud, as well as the mysterious Savannah.

"So Tex locked up the cabin for nearly thirty-five

years. And he gave me permission to open it up and air it out."

She didn't mention anything about romantic table settings or meals to win a man's heart.

"I think I know who Savannah was," Aidan said.

Tammy was all ears. "You do? Who was she?"

"You remember when I broke up with Emily Barfield a few years back?"

She nodded. Emily had been Aidan's very first girlfriend. And they'd split up when he learned she'd been seeing his best friend behind his back.

"I really loved her," Aidan said. "And I took the breakup hard. One day, Dad came in and found me in the den, drowning my sorrows with his best bourbon. I thought he was going to hit the roof. But when I told him about Emily and Todd, he poured himself a drink, too. After a while, he told me that he knew what I was going through. He said he'd fallen hard for a girl while in college. I don't remember her name, since I got bombed that night, but I think it could have been Savannah."

"So what happened?" Tammy asked.

"Like I said, I'm fuzzy on some of the details he shared with me that night. But right before finals, Dad had hitched a ride with a guy from his dorm to attend a party. On the way there, they were involved in a serious car accident. Dad was hurt pretty badly, including several fractures in his leg."

Her father had never told her any of that—not even when she'd asked him point-blank about Savannah just days ago.

"The girl—Savannah, I guess—offered to drive him

back to the ranch, stay with him and nurse him back to health. And Dad was thrilled. He'd been crazy about her, and he was looking forward to introducing her to his dad and his brother.

"Sam came home from college, too. And while Dad was laid up, Sam started showing Savannah around the ranch. I'm not sure how it happened, but Dad learned his brother and Savannah were sleeping together. He was heartbroken and furious."

Wow. Her father had mentioned that Sam had done something unforgivable. And Tammy had connected the dots, thinking that Savannah must have been involved. So this all made sense.

"Did Savannah run off with Sam?" she asked.

"Dad said that Tex flipped out and ran her off the ranch. And to that day…" Aidan chuffed. "Hell, probably until this very day, he's never forgiven his brother or his dad."

"Even after he married our mother?" Tammy asked. She might not have known any of the details from his years spent on the Flying B, but he'd told her all about going to work on Grandpa Murdoch's ranch, where he met her mom, fell in love and got married.

"Dad said Mom was a real sweetheart, and he admitted to marrying her on the rebound. But they had a lot in common—and they were happy."

"You'd think that he would have eventually forgiven his father and even his brother," Tammy said.

"Men shouldn't sleep with the woman a brother—or a best friend—loves."

He was right about that.

"If Nathan had gone after Emily, I might have done

the same thing Dad did. It was bad enough having my friend do it."

Tammy remained silent for a moment, taking it all in, when Aidan placed a hand on her shoulder. "By the way, sis…I meant to tell you that you look great."

She brightened at the compliment. "Oh, yeah? Thanks."

"I wondered if you'd ever turn in those cowgirl clothes for something more womanly." He eyed her carefully. "So what's the deal? Why do I suspect that a man may have triggered the change?"

"Because one did. His name is Dr. Michael Sanchez."

"The guy who went in to see Tex after we came out of the meeting?"

"Yep. What do you think?"

Aidan gave her shoulder a squeeze. "I think he'd better treat my little sister right, or he'll have to answer to me."

Her heart warmed at Aidan's protective streak. "Thanks, but I can take care of myself."

Aidan chuckled. "Yeah, you probably can."

He was talking about putting Mike in his place if he got out of hand or treated her disrespectfully. But the only place Tammy wanted Mike to be was right back in her arms, with his lips locked on hers.

Last night, Tammy had gone to bed thinking about Mike—as if there was anything else to keep her thoughts busy these days. And much to her delight, she'd dreamed that she and Mike had made love in Savannah's cabin.

Music had played softly in the background.

The moonlight had shone through the slats in the blinds, lighting the bedroom in an iridescent and magical glow. A scented candle burned near the bed.

She and Mike had kissed until her knees weakened, then he carried her to the feather bed, where he loved her with his hands, with his mouth until...

Well, until she woke up alone, hugging her pillow.

Too bad she hadn't been sleeping on the feather bed when she'd had that amazing dream, because she would have believed there was a good chance it might actually come true.

She'd love to know that she and Mike were fated to be together—and in the loveliest way possible.

Or had her dream only been a result of wishful thinking?

As much as she'd like to believe that their relationship was destined to blossom, she realized she'd probably have to do her part, too.

And that meant cooking him another dinner in Savannah's cabin. She could light candles, put on some music—maybe even open the slats slightly on the shades to allow the moonlight to spill into the bedroom....

Boy howdy. Just thinking about it had her heart and hopes soaring. So she took a shower, dressed in some work clothes, then headed for the cabin, where she set the stage for an instant replay of the night she'd dreamed about.

For the meal, she decided on grilled chicken, rice pilaf and a garden salad. When she finished the food prep, she washed her hands, then reached for a paper towel. When she was done, she opened the cupboard under the sink to toss the crumpled towel into the trash, only to miss. So she stooped to pick it up.

As she reached for it, she noticed a slip of yellowed paper she hadn't seen before.

An old grocery receipt?

If so, it was too yellowed to be one from any of her shopping trips. Had it been Savannah's?

Out of curiosity, she picked it up and scanned the items on the list: milk, bread, lunch meat, pasta, a... Tammy blinked, thinking she'd misread the last item. But she hadn't.

If the receipt, dated August 29, 1980, had truly been Savannah's, she'd purchased more than food that day. She'd also bought a home pregnancy test kit.

Had the woman who'd slept—okay, *allegedly* slept— with two brothers, gotten pregnant by one of them?

Had either of the Byrd brothers known?

Had an unexpected pregnancy really blown the family sky-high?

Stunned by the possibility, Tammy stood in the small kitchen for what felt like hours. Then she took the receipt and went in search of Jenna.

Since she hadn't been in the house, and Tammy hadn't seen her in the yard, the only place left to look was in the barn.

And sure enough, that's where she found her.

"You spend more time outdoors than you do inside," Tammy said.

Jenna glanced up. "It's more peaceful out here. Not that anything is going on inside, but the silence is intense."

"I think things are going to get worse before they get better."

Jenna furrowed her brow. "Why do you say that?"

Tammy handed her the grocery receipt. "I just found this under the sink in the cabin. I think someone— Savannah—tossed it in the trash, only it fell behind an old scrub brush."

Jenna took the yellowed paper and looked it over. As she undoubtedly reached the last item, she looked up, her lips parted. "You think Savannah was pregnant?"

Tammy shrugged. "There's no way of knowing what results she found, but it sure seems likely that she considered the possibility."

"If so, who was the father?"

Tammy shrugged. It could have been either one.

The furrow in Jenna's brow deepened, and it was easy to see she was troubled by the turn of events.

"From what I've gathered so far," Tammy added, "my dad met Savannah at college, fell in love with her and brought her home to meet his family."

"So it was my dad who slept with his brother's girl-friend?" Jenna asked.

That's the conclusion Tammy had come to days ago, but she hadn't wanted to voice it.

"All we have to go on are rumors," Tammy said. "But assuming both men fell for the same woman, that's probably how it all went down."

Jenna grew silent. After a couple of beats, she said, "We could have another cousin or a sibling out there."

"Yes, but the test could have been negative."

Either way, the family had been torn apart.

"Do you mind if I keep this for a while?" Jenna asked. "I'd like to show it to Donna."

"No. Go right ahead."

"What a mess," she mumbled. Then she tucked the receipt into her pocket and headed for the house.

Tammy followed her as far as the barn door, then she veered to the right and headed for the cabin. While intrigued by the possibility of having another cousin or sibling out there, she was more focused on the romantic evening she had planned for her and Mike.

She'd never lost a prize that she'd set her heart on.

And by hook or by crook, she would woo and win the handsome new doctor.

When Mike left the Flying B, both his heart and his thoughts were heavy. Tex Byrd wasn't going to last much longer, and Mike hoped that the dying man's last wish would come true, that he'd see his family pull together and mend their fences.

Yet Mike thought of Tammy, too. Of her pretty smile, those expressive blue eyes and a petite yet amazing shape that darn near begged to be unveiled and caressed.

If that family meeting hadn't taken place this afternoon, he would have been tempted to stay and have dinner with her again. And maybe, if invited, he might have stayed for breakfast, too.

Did he dare get involved with one of the local women—not that Tammy was from Buckshot Hills. But she was definitely here now, albeit temporarily. And so was he.

His cell phone rang, and he answered using the Bluetooth in the cab of his truck. "Dr. Sanchez."

"Miguel?"

A smile stretched across his face. "Hey, Mom. What's up?"

"Nothing much. I was just thinking about you. We haven't talked in a while. How are you?"

"I'm doing all right. Practicing medicine in a small town is a whole lot different than in the city. It's kind of like stepping back in time—as far as treating patients goes. But it's not so bad."

And it really wasn't. His patients all tended to confide in him, as if he was not only their doctor, but also their friend and neighbor. Like Helen Winslow, who'd sent him home with an apple pie last week. And Marcos Morales, who'd insisted he attend a family barbecue next Sunday.

Mike hadn't told anyone about his plans to leave Buckshot Hills as soon as Stan Reynolds returned to work. So maybe that's why they'd all been so accepting. They didn't realize he was still an outsider.

"Katrina came by to see me the other day," his mother said.

"Oh, yeah?" That struck him as odd. Katrina had always been polite to his mother, but she'd never been very friendly.

"I asked her if she'd heard from you, and she said yes. She also mentioned that she might surprise you one day and fly to Texas."

Mike had thought that he'd talked her out of a visit to Buckshot Hills, which would have only made things worse. She wouldn't appreciate the townspeople, who were a far cry from some of the snooty socialites she ran around with. And more down-to-earth, more honest. More real.

"What else did Katrina have to say?" he asked.

"Just that she missed you terribly. And that she couldn't wait for you to come back home. She also asked if I needed anything. And then she left her phone number and told me to call if I did."

Again, he found that strange—although not if Katrina was actually feeling remorseful about her lack of support when it came to Mike honoring his commitment.

"I might be a thousand miles away, Mom, but if you ever need anything, all you have to do is say the word, and I'll take care of it."

"I'm fine, *mijo*. Mr. Ballard is in Europe, so the house is empty and quiet, which makes my job easy."

He was glad to hear it. She'd always worked hard. And Mr. Ballard, whose house was enormous, entertained a lot.

After the man had agreed to pay for Mike's medical school, his mother had really gone above and beyond, as if trying to pay him back on her own. And he worried about her now. She had a few health issues, like diabetes and high blood pressure, that concerned him.

"When I get home," Mike said, "you can start planning your retirement."

"I've been planning it already—not that I've set any dates yet. I'm just hopeful that my knees will last. The doctor has been talking about replacement surgery, but I'd rather not take the time off to have it done."

"You may not have that option."

"I know. But I'm tougher than you think."

That wasn't true. Mike knew just how strong she was. But she wasn't getting any younger. And she deserved to have a lot more free time to enjoy herself. She'd given up so much over the years.

"Take it easy," he told her. "And don't put off that knee surgery, Mom. I don't like seeing you suffer."

She chuckled. "It's not so bad yet. I'll be okay."

He hoped so. She wasn't one to complain, whether it was from exhaustion, pain or a lack of finances.

"Some things are to be expected as we age," she added.

"Don't start on me about being old, Mom. You've got a lot of good years in front of you. Start thinking about the kind of cruise you'd like to take. I'm sending you on one, just as soon as I get on with the Riverview Medical Group."

"You're too good to me, Miguel."

"No. You're the one who's been too good."

The conversation lagged for a beat, then Mike said, "I'll be back in Philadelphia before you know it."

"That's good to know. I've missed you. Well, I'd better let you go. I've got to get to the post office before it closes. Mr. Ballard is expecting a package."

"All right, Mom. I'll talk to you soon."

When the call ended, he focused on the road ahead, on the jackrabbit that dashed across the street. On the cows that grazed in the grassy field to his right, the cornstalks growing to his left and on the black crows that roosted on the telephone wires overhead.

No, Buckshot Hills was nothing like Philly, which was alive with culture and history. All things considered, he ought to be looking forward to returning home for good.

And he was.

But when it came to counting the days, he couldn't seem to get past one—tomorrow.

When he'd spend the evening with Tammy.

Chapter Ten

Tammy had darn near worn a path through the hardwood floor in the living room, as she paced in front of the window, waiting for Mike to drive up.

Yesterday he'd said that he didn't want to stay while everyone was still reeling from the meeting, and she hoped that he'd feel differently today, especially since the family had already begun to disperse.

Nathan and Aidan, whose construction company had been invited to bid on a big project in Dallas, had left early this morning, saying they needed to submit their proposal.

And as far as her father and uncle went, they'd each taken off, too, but in different directions. No surprise there. But at least they weren't fighting.

Tammy hadn't told anyone about the receipt yet, other than Jenna, who was going to tell Donna. But with Tex coming to the end of his days, there was a lot of emotional stuff to deal with. And Tammy suspected that Savannah's possible pregnancy was the least of their problems. In fact, a revelation like that might prove to make things worse between her father and uncle. So she'd kept quiet about the receipt and spent the bulk of her day getting ready for Mike's arrival, which included a trip into town for propane.

She'd found an old barbecue in one of the outbuildings yesterday and had taken it to the dream cabin and cleaned it up. If her luck held out, the old thing would light right up and she'd grill chicken that had been prepared with her special marinade.

Today, when she'd prepared a salad and rice pilaf, she'd set the table for two. Then she'd returned to the main house and took a second shower of the day. Then she'd put on a skimpy little pair of silky white undies, as well as the matching bra, and slipped into the snug jeans Jenna had insisted she buy—a fancy pair she'd never wear while riding or working on the ranch.

She chose a turquoise top with a scooped neckline to round off her outfit. After brushing her hair, she applied a bit of makeup—some mascara and lipstick. Of course, by now, she'd probably chewed all the color from her lips.

When she finally heard Mike's truck pull into the yard, she did her best to act cool, calm and collected, even though her pulse rate spiked.

Yet in spite of her best intentions, she opened the door before he had the chance to knock.

She greeted him and let him inside, yet she couldn't help allowing her gaze to linger on him.

He wore a pair of black slacks this afternoon and a

pale blue dress shirt, reminding her more of a city doctor and not the kind of man who dedicated his life to treating small-town folk. Yet his dark hair, which was stylishly mussed, whiskey-colored eyes and easy grin suggested he was as down-to-earth as any ol' Buckshot Hills cowboy.

Well, not just any cowboy. One who was as tall, dark and sexy as the good Lord made 'em.

"How's your grandpa doing today?" he asked.

"He's been sleeping a lot the past few hours, but that's probably due to him having quite a few visitors this morning. My brothers each talked to him before they left. And so did my dad and my uncle, which must have taken a lot out of him."

"I'm sure it did." Mike's gaze locked on hers, and her tummy turned inside out. "How about you, Tammy? How are you holding up?"

In truth? She was torn between nagging grief at losing her grandfather before ever having a chance to really get to know him and the thrill of seeing Mike again. But she couldn't very well admit that to him, so she gave a little shrug. "I'm all right. But it's not easy watching him grow weaker each day."

Mike placed his hand on her shoulder in a sympathetic gesture, yet the heat of his touch shot clean through her, warming her to the bone.

The emotion in his eyes, the compassion in his touch, changed something deep inside of her, setting her whole life on hold—and on edge.

Sure, her father and brothers had always been good to her—understanding, too. But never like this.

As a result, whatever feelings she'd thought that she

had for Dr. Mike Sanchez deepened now, shifting from sexual attraction and respect to something more. Something she could pin her heart and dreams on for the rest of her natural born days.

For that reason, she felt as if she could tell him anything, ask him anything. And the whole idea was both comforting and scary at the same time.

After all, she'd never let anyone see the real Tammy before—the heart of the woman she'd kept hidden behind oversize flannel shirts.

Shaking off the momentary vulnerability, she turned her thoughts back on Tex.

"How much longer do you think he has?" she asked.

"My best guess is just days."

Tammy glanced down at her feet and bit her bottom lip, then looked back up at Mike. As she did so, tears filled her eyes and slipped down her cheeks.

For as long as she could remember, she'd done her darnedest not to ever cry in front of anyone, especially those of the male gender. So she swiped at the moisture with the back of her hand, fighting the emotional weakness.

Mike reached out and cupped her cheek, his thumb caressing her skin, his gaze laden with compassion. "I'm sorry you have to go through this."

She wasn't sure how to respond. A thank-you didn't seem to work—to be enough. Instead, she just stood there, her eyes locked on his, as some kind of invisible bond formed between them. Something tangible. Something…promising.

Mike's fingers trailed down her cheek as he lowered his arm. "I'd better go check on him."

Yes, he should. Yet neither of them moved for the longest moment, as if he was as reluctant to let go and step away as she was.

"I have dinner cooked," she said. "If you're hungry."

"In the cabin?"

Where else could she have him all to herself? She nodded, her heart rate pounding to beat the band.

"All right. I'll meet you there."

Perfect. Just as she'd hoped. Just as she'd dreamed, just as she'd planned.

As Mike headed for the hallway that led to Tex's bedroom, Tammy left the house through the kitchen, taking time to snatch one of the peanut butter cookies Barbara had baked to eat on the run.

At one time, she thought she was destined to live on her daddy's ranch the rest of her life—an old maid, a quirky aunt to her brothers' children.

But now, some big changes were on the horizon.

Yet the future never looked brighter.

Mike took one last look at Tex, who was resting easy in spite of the trying day. He hoped the old man had been able to talk to his sons, and that some sort of healing had begun, because he'd grown to care about the dying rancher and his family.

Okay, so the family member Mike cared most about was Tammy. What was he going to do about her?

He wasn't sure if he should put her on a stage and enjoy her unpredictable antics, store her on a shelf so he could step back and admire her from afar, or draw her close and enjoy the ride of his life.

After taking a moment to talk to Tina and give her

instructions to call him on his cell if Tex should take a turn for the worse, Mike left the house and headed toward the cabin. He found himself looking forward to seeing what Tammy had fixed for him tonight, and he kicked up his pace a notch.

By the time he reached the knoll, the sun had slipped low in the west Texas sky, streaking the horizon in shades of pink, orange and gray. Up ahead sat the cabin.

Tammy hadn't set a table on the porch, like she'd done the last time he'd come. He wondered what she had in mind this time. Dinner in the house, he supposed.

He climbed the steps, crossed the small porch then knocked.

When Tammy opened the door, the aroma of whatever she'd cooked snaked around him, taunting him. Yet it was the scent of her spring-fresh perfume and the warmth of her breezy smile that sent his senses reeling. And for the briefest moment he wondered what it might be like to set down roots in Buckshot Hills.

But Mike couldn't do that. He'd worked too hard to give up his dream of practicing cutting-edge medicine.

"Come in," Tammy said, stepping aside. "Dinner's just about ready."

"It sure smells good."

"Thanks. That's just the rice pilaf. I'd planned to grill chicken on the back patio. Why don't you come outside? You can handle the barbecue—if you'd like to. Or I'll do it. No biggie."

He followed her outdoors, where she'd set up the table, along with a candle, a small glass vase of wildflowers and an uncorked bottle of white wine.

"I'll do the grilling," he said. "Why don't you sit down and relax?"

"All right, you've got a deal. The rice is finished. And I have a salad in the fridge. As soon as the chicken is ready, we can eat."

"Next time, I owe you dinner," he said.

"I'd like that."

He realized that implied they were dating. But what would that hurt?

She pointed to a tired old barbecue that had seen better days. "If you want to light the grill, I'll go into the kitchen and bring out the marinated meat."

"Does this thing even work?" he asked.

"I tried it out earlier, and it does. I left the matches on top."

Ten minutes later, as Mike turned the sizzling chicken that cooked on the grill, Tammy poured them each a glass of wine, handed him one then took a seat at the table.

"Do you miss Philadelphia?" she asked.

Not at the moment. And certainly not as much as he had on the day he'd first arrived in Buckshot Hills and studied the small clinic out of which he was supposed to practice medicine.

"I grew up in Philly, so it's been quite an adjustment to live in Buckshot Hills."

"I imagine it is."

Mike turned back to the grill, making sure that the flame wasn't too hot, that the chicken wasn't burning.

"But you do like it here, don't you?"

"Sure." There was plenty to like about Buckshot Hills, if a person was into a slower pace. But Mike was used to a big city, to the cultural opportunities. Not to mention the career opportunities when it came to practicing medicine. But since Tammy was a small-town girl herself, he didn't want her to think he didn't appreciate her way of life.

When the chicken was finished, Mike placed it on a serving dish, while Tammy went into the cabin to bring out the salad and rice. Then they each took a seat at the table.

While the candle burned bright, a lonely cricket chirped. Somewhere a horse whinnied. Overhead, the moon, while not quite full, shone bright.

Mike had to admit that sitting outside on a summer night, with Tammy seated across from him, was an opportunity and a pleasure he wasn't likely to get in the city. Any city.

It almost made a man wish he'd been made for a simpler lifestyle. And it almost caused him to question the belief that he hadn't been.

Tammy lifted her napkin and blotted her lips. "My grandfather is leaving the Flying B to me and my cousins, Jenna and Donna."

"How do you feel about that?"

"I'm honored, actually. And I'm looking forward to working with my cousins. I may have just met them, but I like them. Of course, I don't know Donna nearly as well as I do Jenna, but she seems nice." Tammy took a sip of her wine. "Of course, she's the city-girl type, if you know what I mean. So I'm not sure how she'll feel about settling in Buckshot Hills."

Mike had noticed that about Donna, too. And Tammy was a country girl, through and through.

"Jenna had the idea of turning it into a B and B," Tammy added, "but we haven't really had a chance to talk about it. I mean, it feels weird making plans for the house and property, when Tex isn't even gone yet."

"I can understand that." Mike set his fork down and pushed his plate aside. "You know, Tammy, I have to tell you. A man could get used to having dinner with you every night. You're one heck of a cook."

She damn near beamed at the compliment, those blue eyes sparking in the candlelight. "Thanks."

A beat later, she asked, "How about some ice cream? I thought something simple and light would make a nice ending to a barbecue meal."

"You thought right." Mike stood and gathered the plates. "Come on. I'll help you carry these inside."

Moments later, the table was cleared, and the dishes had been placed on the counter.

"I'll fill the sink with soapy water," Tammy said. "We can let everything soak while we have dessert."

As Mike lifted the plates he'd stacked, a fork fell onto the floor. He bent and reached for it, then placed it into the warm water. As he did so, his hand brushed Tammy's, their fingers touching. Lingering.

Their gazes met and held.

He had no idea what she was feeling, but his breath damn near stopped, his heartbeat, too.

What was it about her that he found so damn appealing, so attractive, so...

So worth pursuing?

He'd be damned if he knew. But nothing seemed to matter, especially the fact that a sexual relationship would only be temporary.

To hell with the dishes.

And with the ice cream.

He didn't even care about any reason he should avoid getting in too deep with one of the locals. Because if Tammy was willing, then he was, too.

He lifted his hand from the sink and turned to face her. As if their bodies were already connected, she turned, too.

They stood like that for a moment, then in spite of having a wet, soapy hand, he reached for her face.

Ignoring the suds on his knuckles, he brushed his thumb across her cheek, making wet, circular motions.

If the dampness bothered her, she didn't let on. Instead, her head tilted and her lips parted, as if she knew how sorely tempted he was to kiss her senseless.

As Mike's gaze searched Tammy's face, as he cupped her jaw, as his wet thumb caressed her skin in a sensuous way, her heart rate slipped into overdrive.

Who would have guessed that warm dishwater could be so darned sexy?

Desire shadowed his eyes, and she sensed he was going to kiss her again. Yet even if he didn't, she would take the bull by the horns and make the first move herself.

"You're not making this easy," he said.

"I'm not the one fighting it."

A grin tugged at his lips. "Then I surrender."

As he lowered his mouth to hers, her heart scampered through her chest, as if looking for a way out. Or maybe it was trying to find a way to let his heart in.

Either way, it didn't matter. And neither did the fact that her hands were still wet.

She slipped her arms around his neck and leaned in for the kiss. Her lips parted, and her tongue sought his, finding it.

As their bodies pressed together, their hands stroked, caressed, explored. All the while, the kiss deepened, intensifying to the point where she could hardly catch her breath. But if truth be told, she'd just as soon turn blue and die in his arms, if she had to.

About the time she thought her knees might turn to mush, he placed his hands on her hips and pulled her flush against his erection.

A surge of desire shot clean through her, creating an ache in her very core, and she nearly cried out with the strength of it all. Somehow catching her breath, she arched forward, revealing her own need, her own arousal.

When he finally drew his mouth from hers, his breathing as ragged as hers, he whispered against her hair. "What do you say? Should we take this into the bedroom?"

For a woman who'd only experienced her first real kiss just days ago, she didn't have a single qualm about taking the next step—as long as it was with Mike. She'd take all he offered her this evening, a single kiss or a whole lot more.

"I'm game if you are," she said.

And she was. Her womanly self-confidence was soaring at an all-time high. And it didn't matter one bit that there wasn't a single tutor in sight. She wouldn't need any coaching from here. Her body responded to

Mike's, as if she'd made love with him a hundred times before.

He brushed his lips against hers one last time, then slipped his hand into hers and led her to the living room. But they barely made a step toward the bedroom when his cell phone rang.

His movements froze, and he swore under his breath.

"Do you have to take that call?" she asked.

"I don't have an answering service, so I have to see who it is. If it's a patient, I'll need to take the call."

Tammy waited for him to answer, watched his brow furrow.

"Is there anyone who can drive you to the hospital in Granite Falls?" Mike asked the caller. Then he nodded, listening to the response. "Okay. Good. I'll meet you there. And don't worry. Everything is going to be fine."

As he disconnected the line, Tammy asked, "What's wrong?"

"Melanie Snyder's water broke. She's still nearly five weeks early, so she's worried. She miscarried a couple of times, and this is her first baby. So even though there'll be an obstetrician who can handle things, I need to go. Her husband isn't around, and I'd like to be there—at least, until he arrives."

"Didn't we drive out to the Snyder ranch to see about Slim and Pete, the hands who fell through the barn roof?" she asked.

"Yes, it's the same ranch."

Tammy thought so. Mike had mentioned something to her about the woman that day. "Could I ride along with you?"

"It might take a while. Granite Falls is more than an hour's drive from here."

"I don't mind."

He waited a beat, as if giving it serious consideration, then smiled. "Sure. Why not?"

As they headed for Mike's truck, Tammy couldn't still a rush of excitement. She liked knowing that she and Mike had become a team, that he wanted her to be with him.

Sure, she'd been disappointed that their romantic evening had ended so abruptly, but that was merely a temporary inconvenience. Next time, Tammy promised herself, they would make it all the way to the bedroom.

She'd make sure of it.

Tammy and Mike arrived at the small hospital in Granite Falls at a quarter to nine. After leaving Tammy in the waiting room, Mike took off to find Melanie Snyder, who'd been admitted and sent to the maternity ward.

As soon as he was gone, Tammy dug through a stack of magazines, finding one. Then she settled into a seat, prepared to wait for hours.

But as luck would have it, Mike returned in less than two.

"How'd it go?" she asked, setting down a crossword puzzle booklet someone had left behind. "Are Melanie and her baby going to be okay?"

"Yes, they're going to be fine. Brian just arrived, so she's got his support now. She's also under the care of the resident obstetrician, who's monitoring the baby. Everything appears to be going well. The doctor was very reassuring, so she's feeling much better. He also told her that at the rate she's going, she'd be holding her son by morning."

"I'm so happy to hear that."

"Me, too. Brian and Melanie are two of the nicest people you'll ever meet." Mike reached out and took her by the hand. "Come on. Let's get out of here."

They left the hospital and headed for the parking lot, still holding hands. A real couple. Teammates.

Imagine that. Never had Tammy been so happy.

"I can drive you back to the ranch," Mike said, as they neared the spot where he'd parked his pickup. "Or, if you'd rather, we can go back to my place and...take up where we left off."

Goodness. She didn't want to sound too eager, too pleased with the suggestion. "I'll stay with you in town. That way, you won't have to drive me all the way back to the Flying B. By the time you got home, you wouldn't get much time to sleep."

"I might not, anyway." He gave her hand a gentle squeeze. "But you won't hear any complaints from me."

Moments later, they were in his truck, heading back to Buckshot Hills. Because of the late hour, there was little traffic on the road, so they made good time. Yet it was still after midnight when they reached city limits.

As they approached the Buckshot Hills Motor Inn and Connie's Country Kitchen, the all-night diner, Tammy realized not everyone in town had turned in. A pink neon no vacancy sign flashed below the motel's sign. And the diner, which sat across the shared parking lot, appeared to be hopping, in spite of the hour.

Two sedans, a pickup and a motorcycle were parked in front. And an eighteen-wheeler was parked in the back.

"Are you hungry?" Mike asked.

"No, I'm fine." She was also eager to get to his place—and to pick up where they'd left off.

They'd no more than passed the diner, when Mike slowed and turned on his blinker. Then he made a right-hand turn onto a tree-lined street. He came to a stop in front of a small, white clapboard house, where a white sedan was parked in the drive, the dome light on.

"I wonder who that is," he said, as he parked at the curb. Before he could shut off the headlights, a tall, shapely redhead got out of the sedan.

Tammy didn't think anything of it—until Mike swore under his breath.

"Do you know her?" she asked.

"Her name's Katrina. And apparently, she decided to surprise me with a visit." Mike blew out a sigh, then raked a hand through his hair. "Do you mind waiting here, Tammy? I need to talk to her privately."

Without waiting for her response, he pulled the keys from the ignition, opened the driver's door and got out of the truck. Then he strode toward the woman.

Tammy had no idea who Katrina was. But by the look on the well-dressed woman's face, she wasn't at all happy to see Mike.

Or rather, to see that he hadn't come home alone.

Chapter Eleven

Katrina nodded her head toward the cab of Mike's pickup. "Who's that woman? And what's she doing with you?"

Mike didn't need to glance over his shoulder to know that Katrina was talking about Tammy, who was waiting in the truck. Or that Tammy was undoubtedly wondering the same thing about her.

"She's the granddaughter of one of my patients," he told his former fiancée.

Katrina lifted her hand, flashing the diamond engagement ring she still wore. The one she'd told Mike she was going to return, yet she hadn't quite gotten around to it.

Apparently she'd decided the engagement was back on. And even though she'd implied as much during their past few phone conversations, Mike certainly hadn't agreed to that.

For all intents and purposes, he and Katrina had split up before he'd even left Philadelphia. For that reason, he didn't feel the least bit guilty about coming so close to making love with Tammy earlier this evening.

Of course, he was feeling pretty damned guilty right now, especially since Tammy had been inadvertently drawn into a touchy situation she hadn't deserved.

"It's so late," Katrina said. "It's after midnight. If, as you say, that woman is related to one of your patients, why did you bring her home with you?"

Mike wasn't sure what he owed Katrina—if anything. But he certainly didn't have anything to explain.

"We've been at the hospital all evening," he said. "And I was giving her a ride home." He didn't mention that they'd decided it was his "home" that she'd be going to, especially when a change of plans was clearly in order now.

Katrina crossed her arms, skepticism splashed across her pretty face. "Are you *sleeping* with her?"

"Listen, Kat. I'm not even going to answer that question. And as a side note, as far as our engagement goes, we broke up before I came to Texas. And while we've had a few telephone conversations, things haven't really changed between us."

She stiffened. "So you're more than friends with that woman you claim is your patient's granddaughter."

"If you want to discuss our engagement, the breakup and any second thoughts you might be having, I'll be happy to talk about it—*after* I get back from running Tammy home. But for the record, my life and my friendships in Buckshot Hills are none of your concern—

especially since it was my temporary move here that caused you to call it quits."

Katrina released a weary sigh. "You're right, Mike. And I'm sorry—about the breakup, about not being more supportive of you, about being hard-headed and selfish. I really do want to talk things over with you, so I'll wait for you to get back." Her shoulders slumped, and she leaned against the rental car. "It's been a long day. So if you don't mind, I'll probably shower and fix something to eat while you're gone."

"Now, wait just one minute, Kat. You can't just show up on my doorstep and expect to camp at my place."

"Actually, that wasn't my plan until I tried to check into that no-tell motel down the street."

"I knew you wouldn't find anything in Buckshot Hills that was up to your standards. That was one of the reasons I told you not to bother coming here in the first place."

There were others, of course. The fact that she was used to five-star hotels, turn-down service and mints on the pillow was a big one, though.

"Besides the fact that the place was so seedy and run-down, it was also *full*. So if you don't mind, I'd like to stay here for the night. The lady at the motel suggested I come back tomorrow, after twelve."

This time, Mike couldn't help glancing over his shoulder at Tammy.

"Dammit," Katrina said. "You're not going to put me out on the street, are you? I've been up since five. And I've had a missed connection, and a two-hour drive just to get here."

He couldn't tell her no. He'd just have to explain to Tammy, to tell her he'd make tonight up to her somehow.

Using the house key that was attached to the fob in his hands, he opened his front door for her and turned on a light.

Katrina, who'd reached into the car and had taken out her suitcase, followed him inside.

"Make yourself at home," he said. "I'll be back in an hour or so."

As Katrina set her suitcase on the hardwood floor, next to the sofa, Mike returned to his pickup. God only knew what Tammy was thinking.

What a fix he was in. He had two women, both deserving a heart-to-heart. And he'd be damned if he knew what to say to either of them.

Yet the one he was most worried about, most invested in, was Tammy.

All the while Mike had been talking to the redhead, Tammy's tummy had tossed and turned. Finally, when he opened the front door and let her carry a suitcase inside, her gut clenched.

Now, as he approached the pickup, his expression solemn, she feared she'd throw up and embarrass herself.

She had no idea why she was so unsettled, when she didn't know who the woman was, but Mike obviously knew her well enough to let her stay with him. And that meant his and Tammy's plans for the rest of the night were out.

Unless, of course, he planned to leave the redhead

here and stay on the Flying B with Tammy. But something told her not to count on that happening.

And, if truth be told, she wasn't so sure she wanted it to.

"I'm sorry," he said, as he opened the driver's door. "Katrina used to be my fiancée. She showed up unexpectedly, and apparently, she'd like to patch things up between us. But it's not that simple."

His fiancée?

"The motel is full, and she had nowhere else to go, so she'll stay here until morning. She and I need to have a talk, so I'll have to drive you back to the ranch."

Just like that? Katrina was in, and Tammy was out?

Everything they'd shared tonight, everything she'd planned, was over.

Tammy's heart began to pound so hard it throbbed in her ears. She wanted to scream, to cuss, to pitch a real fit. But she held her temper and sucked back her tears.

"I'm sorry to drag you into this," Mike said.

Not as sorry as she was. For the first time in her life she had a female rival.

Or was that even the case? After all, Tammy couldn't very well compete for a man who'd never really been up for grabs. And even if she could, the woman—Katrina—had obviously come all the way to Buckshot Hills to patch things up. The two of them had a history—and chemistry, no doubt. So where did that leave Tammy?

Out in the cold, her nose pressed against the locked, fogged-up window to her dreams.

As reality settled over her, her heart ached in a way it never had before. The man she loved belonged to another. And yes, she did love Mike. If she didn't, it wouldn't hurt so badly to lose him.

Okay, so she'd never really *had* him. The belief that she might win his heart had merely been wishful thinking on her part.

And on his part? She'd been a salve to soothe his broken heart, a transitional relationship to help him move on.

Of course, who said he was moving on after his breakup with Katrina? From the looks of it, he was going to be back in her arms by morning.

Just thinking about the two of them together was enough to squeeze the tears right out of her.

Mike reached across the seat and took her hand. "Are you okay?"

Heck no, she wasn't okay. What did he expect from her?

But it wasn't in her nature to show weakness, so she feigned a smile. "Of course. Why wouldn't I be?"

He gave her fingers a gentle squeeze. "Thanks for being so patient. Just give me a few more minutes. I need to get Katrina settled, then I'll take you home."

He needed to get her *settled*?

Hell's bells. It sounded as if Katrina was going to be staying with Mike for God only knew how long.

Emotion balled up in Tammy's throat, threatening to choke the living daylights out of her if she didn't scream out in anger and frustration. But she did her best to swallow it down and to feign a casual smile.

"Thanks for understanding," Mike added. "I won't be long."

The phony smile lingered on her lips. "Take all the time you need, Mike."

Yet in spite of her gracious response, she had absolutely no intention of waiting around for him to tell her that all her dreams of love and romance had just gone up in smoke.

Nor would she just sit in his pickup, twiddling her thumbs until he came back outside and drove her back to the Flying B. She had more pride than that.

She also had cash in her purse.

And she knew right where she'd go. At the diner, she could call a cab. Or she could hire someone to drive her back to the Flying B.

"You take the bed," Mike told Katrina, as he pulled fresh sheets and towels from the linen closet. "I'll camp out on the sofa when I get back."

"I understand your reluctance to jump into anything right away," she said. "But I'd hoped we could just kiss and make up."

"It's not that simple, Kat." He handed her the bedding, as well as a washcloth and towel.

"Would you rather I slept in the car?"

"Don't be ridiculous." He shot another gaze her way.

Her eyes had a glossy sheen, as if she was just one blink away from tears. "I'm sorry for just showing up like this. But I couldn't help it. We weren't making much headway over the telephone, and I wanted to talk to you face-to-face."

Mike paused for a beat, then agreed. "You've got a point, Kat. A discussion is long overdue. But it'll have to wait until I get back."

"All right. But I want you to know that Daddy called in some favors. And Riverview Medical Group is going to hold a spot open for you."

Mike tensed. Before leaving for Texas, he'd talked to the RMG director, Dr. David Goldman, himself. David hadn't made any promises, but he hoped they'd be able to hold the position for Mike, based upon his credentials and letters of recommendation. And while it was nice of Katrina's father to go to bat for him, it felt more like interference than help.

That in itself helped to diffuse some of his frustration and resentment—although just a bit.

"Can I fix something for you to eat while you're gone?" Katrina asked. "I'm not sure what you have for me to work with, but I'll figure out something—even if it's an omelet or canned soup."

Mike wasn't hungry, although it had been a while since he'd had dinner. "Don't go out of your way for me. But if you decide to heat something, the igniter on the stove isn't working. The gas turns on, but you'll need to light the flame. I've got a box of matches in the drawer to the right of the kitchen sink."

He pointed out the cupboard where he kept his pots and pans, as well as the pantry, which didn't have much food in it. "I'd planned to pick up a few groceries in the morning."

"I don't suppose you have any tea," she said.

He'd always kept a variety for her at his place, back in Philly. But he hadn't seen any point in stocking up on her food preferences or her favorite drinks here. Why would he? He'd never expected her to make the trip to Texas in the first place.

"No, I'm afraid I don't," he said. "But I have coffee in the pantry. Creamer, too." He glanced at his watch, eager to get back to the truck. He hated keeping Tammy waiting.

Before he could excuse himself, his cell phone rang. And for a moment, he welcomed the interruption— even though the late-night hour suggested it might be an emergency.

How was that for luck? Just what he needed tonight, another fire to put out.

"This is Dr. Sanchez," he said, upon answering.

"Doc, it's Tina at the Flying B. Tex has taken a turn for the worse. Can you come out here?"

"Of course. I'll be there as soon as I can." When he disconnected the line, he turned to Katrina. "I need to go."

"So what's the matter? Did she call you and ask you to hurry up?"

"Excuse me?"

"The woman in the truck," Katrina said, crossing her arms. "Is she getting tired of waiting for you?"

Mike chuffed. "That call wasn't from the woman in my truck. Actually, I just got word that one of my patients is dying. So I need to go."

Katrina didn't appear to be buying his story, even though it was the truth.

"I don't have time for this," Mike said, as he headed for the door.

Katrina was jealous now?

Maybe she should have worried about losing him to another woman when they'd first discussed his commitment to come to Buckshot Hills.

After leaving Katrina in the kitchen, Mike headed outside to his pickup, only to find the cab empty and Tammy gone.

His heart dropped to the pit of his stomach. Where in the hell had she gone?

A slip of paper had been stuck under the windshield wiper. A note?

Mike opened the driver's door to turn on the dome light so he could read what she'd written in lipstick.

Don't bother taking me back to the ranch. I'll find a ride or call a cab.

Oh, for Pete's sake. What more could go wrong tonight? And where did Tammy think she'd she find a ride at this hour? The town had shut down—other than that diner on Elm.

Mike climbed into the pickup, started the engine and made a U-turn. Then he headed down the street, his headlights on high beam, his eyes peeled on the side of the road for a woman on foot.

When he reached the diner, he parked out front, then went inside and asked if anyone had seen a woman wearing black denim jeans and a turquoise top.

"Was she a pretty lil' brunette in her mid-twenties?" a man seated at the counter asked. "About five foot nothin', but every bit a woman?"

That could only be Tammy. So Mike nodded.

"She hired a trucker to take her home. You just missed 'em."

"A *trucker?*" What had she been thinking? Didn't she know how risky it was to get a ride from a stranger?

His expression must have announced his concern, because one of the waitresses chuckled. "Don't worry.

It wasn't just any ol' trucker. Your friend caught a ride with Mary Jane Baumgartner, who's been driving eighteen-wheelers for years. Mary Jane will get her home safe and sound."

Mike thanked the waitress, then returned to his pickup and headed to the Flying B.

Twenty minutes later, as he turned onto the road that led to the ranch, he passed a big rig on its way back to town. He was relieved to know that, apparently, Tammy had gotten home safely. But he still had half a notion to tell her that catching a ride with a stranger, even a woman, was a half-baked idea.

Mike continued on to the house, which had nearly every light turned on. He assumed the family had gathered at Tex's bedside, and he hoped that the old rancher's passing would be quick and peaceful.

After parking and making his way to the wraparound porch, he rapped lightly on the door. Moments later, Tina, the housekeeper, answered and invited him inside.

"Thanks for coming, Doc." The fifty-something housekeeper blotted her eyes with a damp, wadded tissue.

"Am I too late?"

"No, but it won't be much longer."

He scanned the living room, where the Byrd family had gathered. But he didn't see Tammy among them.

Had he been wrong about her taking a cab home? His gut clenched. "Is Tammy here?"

"Yes, she's with Tex now. But you go right on in. He's already talked to the others."

"Is he in pain?" Mike asked.

"He doesn't appear to be."

"Good."

Mike didn't take time to greet anyone. Instead, he headed down the hall. When he reached Tex's bedroom, the door was open.

Tammy stood at the old man's bedside, holding his hand. Upon hearing Mike's approach, she glanced over her shoulder. They barely made eye contact, when she turned to her grandfather. "Doc is here, now. I'll get out of the way so he can talk to you."

Tex, whose eyes were closed, didn't respond.

As Tammy passed Mike in the doorway, he caught her hand. "We need to talk."

"Why?" She smiled, yet it held none of the warmth and spark he'd grown to expect. "There's nothing to talk about."

He would have argued with her, but he let it go for now and made his way to Tex's bedside, where he assessed his patient's condition.

Tina had been right.

Moments later, Mike watched as Tex drew his last breath. The cantankerous old patriarch who'd wanted to see his family pull together was gone, his last wish fulfilled—at least, somewhat.

Mike went out into the living room, where the Byrds had gathered. "He's gone."

Sam was the first to slip out of the room and go outside, followed by William. For a moment, Mike suspected they'd embrace in grief—or at least say something. Instead, they went off in opposite directions.

Tammy followed her father.

Mike stuck around for a while, waiting for Tammy

to return. But when the mortuary came for Tex's body, she still hadn't come back to the house.

At the break of dawn, he walked out to the cabin to look for her, but she wasn't there.

It wasn't until he started back for the ranch that he noticed her Chevy S-10 pickup was gone.

Mike took a deep breath, then raked his hand through his hair. He had two women to talk to. And while he'd been determined to speak to Tammy first, it didn't look like he would have that opportunity.

He stayed until the sun began its rise over the Flying B, but she'd yet to return. So he drove back to town, where Katrina waited.

Tammy sat behind the wheel of her parked pickup and watched the sunrise. It was amazing how someone could die and a romance could crash and burn— all within the space of an hour—yet life as one knew it went on, the sun continued to shine.

It was nearly seven now, if the clock on her dash was right. She couldn't continue to sit on the side of the county road, staring out the bug-splattered windshield. But she was in no hurry to go anywhere.

After her grandfather's passing, she'd just needed to go outside, to get some fresh air, to find some private time to grieve—for both Tex's death and for Mike's betrayal.

Okay. She had to admit that Mike hadn't actually betrayed her in the sense that her uncle had betrayed her father. After all, she and Mike hadn't even gotten around to making a commitment to each other. But Tammy had already married the man in her heart, and as far as she was concerned, the proclamations of love, a little gold band and vows were only a formality.

God, how could she be so stupid, so naive?

About the time she was going to kick herself for dreaming the impossible, she shook off the urge to beat herself up about it. Why should she, when Mike was the one who forgot to mention that he had a fiancée?

Sure, he might have said that he and Katrina "used to be" engaged, but she still wore his ring. Tammy had seen it glimmer and shine in the glow of the porch light.

How low-down could a man get?

Well, apparently, as low-down as her uncle, when he'd slept with her father's girlfriend.

Before last night, Tammy had only been able to imagine the pain her father had gone through when he'd found out about Savannah and Sam. And now she knew firsthand how he felt.

Well, at least, she had a much better idea.

And that's why, when her father had gone outside after Mike announced Tex's passing, Tammy had followed him out the door and to his restored 1975 Trans Am.

"How're you doing?" she'd asked, when she finally caught up with him.

"Not so good."

Her heart ached for him. He'd lost his father, and she knew how badly she would feel if she were to lose hers. And how much worse it would be to think she'd wasted thirty-five years staying away from him.

"I promised Dad that I'd try to put the past behind me," he said, "but forgiving Sam is going to be tough."

She supposed, after more than thirty years of letting anger simmer into bitterness, it would be.

"I know about Savannah," she said. "And I understand why you're so mad at him."

Her father tensed, then his shoulders slumped. "I loved your mom, Tam. Don't ever think that I didn't. But just because I found someone later and married her, doesn't mean that I was able to forgive or forget what my brother did."

"If Sam was the one who wronged you, why did you stay away from Tex?"

"Because he's the one who lit into Savannah, calling her names, making her the villainess. I've always felt that if I'd gone to Savannah, talked to her, that I could have… Well, that things might have been different. But Dad chased her off, and as a result, she ran away." Her father paused, brow furrowed. "No, that's not true. It's as if Savannah vaporized. I know, because I tried to find her and couldn't."

"Have you forgiven Tex?"

"I told him I did when I first got here. And then again tonight."

"Did you mean it?"

He paused for the longest time. "Yeah, I guess I did."

She pondered the latest piece in the puzzle, wondering if it would be wise to withhold the information about a possible pregnancy. But maybe too much had been kept secret for way too long.

"I have to tell you something, Dad. While cleaning out the cabin Savannah had stayed in, I found an old grocery store receipt. And one of the items purchased was a home pregnancy test."

He jerked back, as if she'd slapped him. Then he raked a hand through his hair. "No kidding?"

"I wouldn't joke about something like that. Of course, just because I found a receipt doesn't mean it was Savannah's. Or, if it was hers, that the results had been positive."

He glanced up at the night sky, at the stars, as if imploring God to step in and fix a mess that only seemed to grow stickier.

"What are you going to do?"

"About Savannah? Not a damn thing."

"What if she was pregnant? What if—"

Her dad placed his hand on her shoulder and gave it a squeeze. "Let it go, Tam. I'm going to have a hard enough time forgiving my brother as it is. If she took off, pregnant, I might never forgive Sam. Or my dad."

Then he pressed a kiss against her cheek. "I gotta get out of here for a while. The past is closing in on me, and I need some fresh air—and some perspective."

"I understand, Daddy. I love you."

"Love you, too, honey." He placed his hand on her cheek, his eyes lingering on hers until they glistened. Then he brushed a kiss on her cheek and turned away.

She thought about calling him back, but she let him climb into his car and rev the engine. As he pulled away, she noticed Mike's pickup.

Earlier tonight, she'd sat in the cab, watching him talk to Katrina, wishing she could hear what was being said. Then he'd returned to the truck, his expression somber.

Wait here, he'd told Tammy, before going into the house to help Katrina "get settled."

But Tammy never had liked following orders, especially a man's. So she'd offered a lady trucker fifty dollars to drive her out to the Flying B.

Then, when she'd passed Mike in the doorway of Tex's bedroom, he'd mentioned it again. *We need to talk.*

She'd told him there was nothing to talk about at the time, but there really was. She'd like to give him a piece of her mind—if she could figure out a way to do it without cussing, and stomping, and spitting. Or without falling apart like a baby.

So that's why she'd gotten into her pickup at that time and had driven off. And it was why she was now waiting to return to the Flying B until she was sure he was gone.

But if he was no longer on the ranch, that meant he'd gone back to Katrina.

She slammed her hand on the dash and blew out a sigh. Then she started the ignition, pulled back onto the road and drove to the Flying B.

Did she dare hope that she'd find him waiting for her?

When she arrived, Mike was gone. Her heart stung at the thought of where he'd gone.

Still, his vehicle wasn't the only one missing. It seemed that her uncle and father had gone, too.

Upon entering the living room, she found Jenna and Donna seated on the sofa. Tina and Barbara sat across from them. They each held either a coffee mug or a teacup.

"I guess we should start thinking about the services," Jenna said.

Barbara shook her head. "That won't be necessary.

Tex wanted to be cremated without any fuss and fanfare."

"What about a celebration of life," Tammy said, as she joined the women. "It doesn't seem right to just…"

She caught herself, thought over what she was about to say. That it didn't feel right to forget that Tex had ever lived.

But wasn't that what her father and uncle had done? Driven off the ranch and refused to return, just as if he'd died thirty-some years ago?

"Tex was very specific about that," Tina said. "He's got it all laid out in his will. He doesn't want anything other than a quiet, graveside service until both of his sons have buried the hatchet."

That just might take a long time, Tammy thought. Especially if there was another Byrd out there somewhere.

Tina smiled, then set down her coffee mug. "I can still remember what he said. 'Tell 'em I don't want any false sentiments. When they can finally put the past to rest—and appreciate at least a couple of good things I did as their father—then y'all can have a big party. But there isn't a damn thing to celebrate on the Flying B until that happens. Otherwise, I'll go down in the annals of family history as a failure.'"

But what if the feud never did get patched up? Tammy wondered.

"By the way," Barbara added, "Darren Culpepper, his attorney and friend, will be coming by at the end of the week to have the formal reading of the will. But from what I heard, it's laid out just the way Tex told you during that meeting you had."

Before anyone could respond, Tina got to her feet. "I don't know about you girls, but I'm exhausted. I'm going to try and get some sleep."

"I was just thinking the same thing," Barbara said, as she stood.

When the older women left the room, Jenna turned to Tammy. "How are you holding up? I know we just met Tex recently, but you were probably the one who was closest to him."

Tammy opened her mouth to explain, but the words jammed in her throat and tears welled in her eyes.

Jenna set down her teacup. "I'm sorry, Tammy. I know how badly it hurts to lose someone you love. But at least we finally got the chance to meet him, to know him."

"It's not Tex." Tammy sniffled. "I mean, it *is*. I feel sad about that, too. But it's more than that." She went on to tell her cousins that her scheme had backfired, that she lost the man she loved.

Jenna stood, crossed the room and enveloped Tammy in a warm embrace. "I'm so sorry. Just know that you have me."

"You have me, too," Donna said. "You know what they say about Byrds of a feather."

They flock together. Somewhat warmed at the thought, Tammy managed a smile. "Thanks, you guys. I'm glad we found each other."

Still she feared her heart would never mend, that she'd never fall in love again.

"You know," Donna said, as she got up from the sofa, "I need to turn in, too."

"Good idea." Jenna lowered her arms and took a step back.

"Ditto," Tammy said. "And even though I don't know if I can sleep, I'd better give it a try."

As she headed for the front door, Jenna stopped her. "Where are you going, Tammy?"

"To the cabin. I need some time alone."

Jenna nodded, clearly understanding.

But what she didn't know was that Tammy hoped to fall asleep in the feather bed and to pray for a dream that would tell her what the future would bring.

Because unless there was some kind of miracle in the works, her future wouldn't include Mike.

Chapter Twelve

Late that afternoon, Tammy woke with a start. It took her a moment to remember where she was—napping on the feather bed in Savannah's cabin.

She blinked a couple of times and rubbed her eyes, trying to orient herself after a visit to dreamland.

Dreamland.

Now that was interesting. She'd had a dream, all right. But since neither she nor Mike were in it, she realized that her future was still just as uncertain as it had been hours ago, before she'd placed her head on the pillow and dozed off.

As she climbed from the bed, she began to straighten the coverlet. While she'd slept, she'd dreamed of a little dark-haired girl, who'd been sitting on top of this very bed. Her darling cherub face was a sweet, gooey mess, yet she continued to reach into a heart-shaped candy box and shove chocolates into her mouth.

She'd only had on a pair of pink panties and matching ribbons tied on her pigtails.

In the distance, a woman's voice called, "Bella Rose! Where are you? Did you run off with Mama's candy?"

The child's eyes, as blue as the Texas sky, grew wide, and her mouth formed an O. She quickly plopped onto her tummy and wiggled off the bed.

Once her pudgy little legs hit the floor, she scampered off, leaving the heart-shaped box and a scatter of half-bitten chocolates on the bed.

And then Tammy woke up.

While the child had been darling, she hadn't seen any recognizable faces or heard any voices that made her believe that mere remnant of a dream had anything to do with her and Mike's future.

But what had she truly expected? That miracle vision she'd hoped would provide a clue of what was to come?

As she left the bedroom, she froze in her steps.

Rather than a revelation of the future, had that dream been a vision of the past?

The child eating candy actually resembled photos of Tammy as a little girl—before her mother had died.

Was that the "Mama" whose Valentine chocolates had been snatched by a two-year-old thief?

Maybe. But neither Tammy nor her mom had ever stepped foot on the Flying B. Why the feather bed? Why this particular cabin?

As her sleep-dazed mind scrambled to make sense of the unexplainable, she continued to walk through Savannah's cabin....

Wait, Tammy thought, as she pulled up again.

Had the dream been about Savannah's child? A little girl who resembled Tammy?

Goodness. Had Tammy's dad been the one to father Savannah's baby? Had Savannah been pregnant with her father's baby when she left the ranch—and *not* Sam's?

It was certainly possible—if the legend of the feather bed was true. And if so, did Tammy have a half sister named Bella Rose?

Why else would the child resemble Tammy?

As she pondered the questions her dream had triggered, she remembered something Tex had told her.

You look a lot like your grandma did. Her hair was dark like yours. And her eyes were nearly the same shade of blue.

And, Tex had added, her name had been Ella Rose Byrd.

Ella?

Bella?

Oh, for Pete's sake. Interpreting that dream, as fragile as it had been, was fruitless. It could have meant anything—or maybe even nothing at all.

Actually, when push came to shove, Tammy would be far better off focusing on what she was going to do about Mike. Because in spite of wanting to avoid him, she wouldn't be able to do that forever, especially if she was going to move to the Flying B and become a permanent resident of Buckshot Hills.

Maybe it was time to pull up her big-girl panties and face the music. She couldn't go on hiding forever, even if it seemed like the most natural thing in the world to do.

After all, Tex Byrd and his sons had hidden their true feelings from themselves and each other for longer than Tammy had been alive. Heck, Tex hadn't even gone after his sons and attempted a reconciliation until he'd learned he was going to die.

And Tammy was no different.

All her life, she'd hidden her feminine side behind flannel and denim. And she'd never told anyone how much she loved fiddling around in the kitchen for fear she'd be banished from riding and roping forever.

More recently, she'd run away from Mike, hiding her feelings, refusing to hear him out.

We need to talk, Mike had told her on two separate occasions.

And he'd been right.

The hiding had to stop before it became a way of life for her, too. That meant she had to lay it all on the line. She had to tell Mike that she'd set her sights on him on day one, that she'd gone out of her way to win his heart and that, along the way, she'd fallen in love with him.

Then she'd have to see how the truth played out.

If he told her he and Katrina had decided to patch things up, it was going to hurt like the dickens. She'd probably even break down and cry.

But Tammy couldn't allow herself to fall into the same type of crippling pattern as the other Byrds had relied on to deal with their pain, their anger.

That meant she would have to find Mike and have that little talk he'd wanted to have.

Before Tammy could take a second step across the living room floor, someone rapped at the cabin door.

When she answered and spotted Mike on the porch,

her breath caught and her heart nearly fluttered out of her chest.

"I've been looking for you," he said.

She really wasn't surprised. He'd been pretty insistent about that talk they needed to have. And she was in a much better mood to have it now than she'd been before.

"Come on in."

It was time to face the music.

And the man who held her heart and her dreams in his hands.

Mike hadn't been sure what to expect from Tammy when he finally found her, but he hoped that her inviting him inside the cabin was a good sign.

"Do you want something to eat or drink?" she asked.

He hadn't eaten since dinner last night, and she was a great cook, so he was tempted to say yes. Instead, he said, "Maybe we'd better get a few things out of the way first."

"All right." She pointed to the small sofa. "Why don't you have a seat?"

When he complied, she took the chair.

He started by saying, "I want you to know how sorry I am about what happened last night. I had no idea that Katrina would show up unannounced."

"I'm sorry, too, Mike. I took off like a spoiled child, and I should have waited for you. Then after Tex died, I should have stuck around again, but I… Well, I guess I just bolted."

"Emotions were high for a lot of reasons."

She glanced at the clasped hands in her lap and bit

down on her bottom lip, as if struggling with something. Then she looked up, seeking his gaze. "Can I go first?"

He wasn't sure what she was getting at.

"I need to say something before you apologize or explain. It's important for me to… Well, it's just important, that's all."

Was she planning to end things before he had a chance to say his piece?

"I love you, Mike. In fact, I never understood the concept of falling in love at first sight until I met you."

The weight of her words, the emotional impact, the sincerity in those pretty blue eyes and the magnitude of what she was offering him damn near knocked the words right out of him.

Of all the things she could have confessed, loving him had come out of the blue. Was he ready to make a bold confession like that?

Every analytical fiber of his being, every rational thought, insisted that it was too much, too fast, too soon. That his feelings, instincts and desires couldn't be trusted until tested by time. Yet there was something else going on inside of him, something too strong to discredit.

Before he could respond, she continued to lay her heart on the line. "I worried that I was too country for you, too backward. After all, I was raised on a working cattle ranch by my tough-as-nails father, and I grew up emulating my big brothers. I never had many female friends or relatives—and I really didn't want any. But when I saw you, something changed inside me. Suddenly, yearnings and longings and dreams I'd never admitted to having rose up, and I was determined to become the woman you deserved. And while I didn't have a clue as to how to go about that, I knew I had to give it my best shot. So I asked Jenna to help me, and…" She waved her hand in front of her. "Well, this is what you get. I'm not citified, like the women you're used to. And I'm not nearly as pretty—"

He stopped her right there. "Slow down, honey. I need to set you straight about that. Without a doubt, you're the most amazing, appealing and attractive woman I've ever met. And not only that, you're as unpredictable as they come, which means that my life will never be boring as long as you're in it."

As the words rolled out of him—heartfelt and true—reality struck hard. *He loved her, too.*

The scientifically trained side of him went on sabbatical, and he knew any questions he might have had, any reservations, were gone.

"More importantly," he added, "you have a pure heart, Tammy. What more could a man ask for in a woman?"

Her eyes welled with tears. She swiped at them with both hands and grimaced. "I knew this was going to happen."

"You know *what* would happen?"

"That spilling out my heart was going to make me get all blubbery." She sniffled, then heaved a sigh.

Mike stifled a full-on grin. "You say that like it's a bad thing."

"It isn't?" She looked at him, her cheeks damp and flushed, her eyes watery.

"Absolutely not. Who doesn't like seeing someone express honest emotion?"

Again, she sniffled. "Does that mean that you might, maybe, care about me a little?"

Mike slowly shook his head. Tammy was one of a kind, a woman to treasure. And she didn't realize it.

When he glanced back at her and saw the doubt dancing with hope in her eyes, he realized it was time to level with her, too.

"Care about you a *little?*" He chuckled. "I can't say that it was love at first sight on my part, although I have to admit, when you met me at the door wearing that sexy black dress, I had a real *wow* moment. But for a guy who'd always believed that love grew slowly over time, it happened pretty darn fast for me. In fact, it's still growing strong. I'm in over my head, honey. And it scares the hell out of me because I never planned on staying in Buckshot Hills. I'd only agreed to cover for Doc Reynolds until he finished his medical treatment."

"And *now?*" she asked.

"I gave him a call this morning and told him I'd stay as long as necessary—and to tell him I'd like to work with him as an associate, if he was willing."

"No *kidding?* What did he *say?*"

"He was actually pleased to hear it. His treatment is going well, but his full recovery is still in question. He wants to take some time to himself, do a little fishing and maybe even see the world. And if the folks in Buckshot Hills have a doctor to look out for them, he'd be happy to turn over his practice to me."

"That's wonderful." Her smile slowly faded, and silence filled the room. Finally, she asked, "What about Katrina?"

"That's what I'd meant to tell you at the beginning of our conversation. When she showed up in town last night, the motel was full and she had no other place to go and I reluctantly let her stay at my place. As soon as I got back from the Flying B, I put on a pot of coffee. Then I woke her up to have the heart-to-heart chat we should have had months ago. Our engagement is over—and it has been ever since I arrived in Texas. She realizes that, too, and knows it's for the best. And…" Mike glanced at his wristwatch. "As we speak, she's on a flight bound for Philadelphia."

A grin stretched across Tammy's lips, dimpling her cheeks. "While I'm being honest with my feelings, I suppose I ought to tell you that I'm really glad she's gone."

Mike returned her smile. "I'm sure you are. I'm glad she went home, too. I'm also glad we were able to talk about our breakup. And not just to put the past behind me. It helped me sort through the future, too."

"In what way?"

"I found myself defending the small-town life and the people of Buckshot Hills. And I began to realize just how much I've grown to care for my patients." And just how much he'd come to care for Tammy. "After Katrina left, I showered, then tried to get some sleep."

"I hope you got some rest. You never know when someone will get sick or hurt and need you."

"I laid down on the sofa around nine and crashed. But the weirdest thing happened. I had a dream that really got me to thinking about you and me and the future."

"A *dream?*" Tammy was on the edge of her seat, bright-eyed and intense. "Tell me about it."

He nearly told her it wasn't important, but she certainly seemed interested. So he said, "I don't put much stock in those kinds of things, but I dreamed that you and I were happily married, with three kids and living in Buckshot Hills."

"Three kids?" Her eyes lit up, as if the thought pleased her immensely.

But why wouldn't it? The whole idea pleased him, too.

"Yep. In my dream, we had two boys and a dark-haired little girl who was the spitting image of you. She was about two years old and as cute as a bug. We named her Bella Rose—after my mom."

Tammy's smile faded. "Your mother's name is Bella Rose?"

"No, it's actually Isabella."

Tammy got up from the chair, joined Mike on the sofa and took his hand in hers. "You're not going to believe this, but I had a dream about that same little girl while sleeping in the feather bed. And legend has it that those dreams are supposed to come true."

"But I wasn't even at the cabin. I was home, sleeping on my sofa."

"Yes, but I slept in the feather bed. And we had connecting dreams. Either way, I know that you and I are meant to be. And that one day, we're going to have a little girl named Bella."

"I hope we do."

She laughed. "But do me a favor. Don't give me chocolates for Valentine's Day while she's a toddler.

She's going to run off with them and make a terrible mess."

Mike squeezed her hand. "I don't believe in magical beds, but you're my dream come true." Then he stood, drew her to her feet and took her in his arms. The love he'd just admitted to having filled his heart to the brim. "I don't know about you, but as far as I'm concerned, we have some unfinished business."

"We certainly do." Her eyes sparked, and she wrapped her arms around his neck and drew his lips to hers.

The kiss began slowly, as if they had the rest of their lives before them. And they truly did.

As their tongues met and mated, their hands stroked, caressed, explored until Mike thought he might explode with desire. He finally removed his lips from hers and whispered against her hair, "What do you say? Think it's time that we finally made that move to the bedroom?"

"I *do*." Tammy took him by the hand and led him to the feather bed she claimed was magical.

And maybe it was. Because whatever Mike was feeling for Tammy, whether she was in his arms or only on his mind, went far beyond the ordinary.

After Tammy pulled back the coverlet, she turned to Mike and began to remove her clothes. He watched as she unbuttoned her jeans and slid the zipper down, as she peeled the denim over her hips and slipped out of them. Next, she removed her blouse and stood before him in a pair of lacy pink panties and a matching bra.

Had another woman ever been so beautiful, so arousing?

"I love you, Tammy."

"I love you, too. In fact, so much it scares me."

"Don't be afraid." He kissed her again, long and thorough. Then he removed his own clothing. As he did, he remembered her implying that she'd been a novice about dating and paused for a beat. "Have you done this before?"

She slowly shook her head.

He was her first? The realization that she was offering him her virginity touched him to the core, and he vowed to cherish that amazing gift for the rest of his life.

"I'll probably fumble through this," she said, "but I'm a quick learner."

Mike laughed and took her in his arms, his hands stroking the slope of her bare back, the curve of her hips. "Honey, you're going to do all the teaching tonight. Just tell me what feels good, what feels right. And I'll take it from there."

"You mean I get to call the shots?"

"Tonight?" He smiled. "Every single one."

She skimmed her fingernails across his chest, sending a shiver through his veins and a rush of heat through his blood.

"Damn," he said. "You *are* a fast learner."

Still, he'd take things slow and easy. They had the rest of the night to make love, and he planned to use every minute of it.

They kissed again, long and deep. When they came up for air, he removed his shirt. All the while she watched him, her eyes bright with love and longing.

As he reached for his belt buckle, she removed her

bra, revealing her beautiful breasts and awakening every nerve ending, every cell in his body.

Finally, when they were both lying naked on the bed and aching with need, he entered her. She flinched and tensed momentarily, but as her body responded to his, the world stood still, and nothing else seemed to matter.

As Mike reached a peak, Tammy let go. Together they shared an earth-shaking, star-spinning climax.

Talk about magic.

But in spite of what Tammy might think, the feather bed didn't have anything to do with it.

Love did.

On Saturday afternoon, the air was heavy—and awkward—as Tammy and the other heirs sat in the living room at the Flying B, listening as Darren Culpepper, Tex's silver-haired attorney, repeated everything Tex had already told them himself.

Just as Tex had explained, he'd also bequeathed money to a ranch hand. Tammy had assumed he'd meant Hugh, but that wasn't the case. The hand who'd been like a son to him was Caleb Granger.

The only real surprise was the amount Tex had given Caleb: one hundred thousand dollars.

"I have a question," Aidan said. "Just who *is* Caleb Granger?"

"A young man who came looking for work and found a home with Tex," Darren said.

"And where is he?" Nathan asked. "Shouldn't he be here at the reading of the will?"

"Caleb had to take a leave of absence because of

family business," Tammy said, remembering what he'd told her right before he left.

Nathan chuckled. "Why didn't I just ask you, Tam. You have the inside track on everything." He turned to Jenna and Donna and winked. "In our family, if we want to know anything, it's standard procedure to ask our little sister first. She either has the answer or knows someone else who does."

"Very funny." Tammy crossed her arms and feigned annoyance, although she hadn't let her brother's good-natured teasing bother her. The truth of the matter was, she did have a curious streak. And she had ways of finding out the information she wanted.

At that point, Darren placed his paperwork into his briefcase and stood. "If you have any questions, please give me a call. Tex wasn't just a client, he was a friend."

Sam stood. "I'll walk you out. I'm taking off, too." Then, after a quick goodbye to his daughters, he followed the attorney outside.

"Well," Aidan said, as he, too, got to his feet, "now that the formalities are over, Nathan and I have to go. There's a big job coming up in Ferris Valley, and if we don't get our bid together and in on time, we'll lose out on the opportunity of our lives."

"Take care," Tammy said, giving each of her big brothers a hug. "I'll see you later."

"Be good to Doc," Aidan said.

"I will." Tammy was glad that her brothers thought highly of Mike. Her dad did, too. They'd all gone to dinner last night, after the men in her family arrived at the ranch. And Mike had not only picked up the tab, but also made his intentions known.

Tammy's dad got up from his seat in the far corner and crossed the room. "Good luck," he told the boys. "I hope you snag that contract."

They thanked him, almost in unison, then headed outside as their father trailed behind them.

Tammy wondered if her dad and her uncle would talk while they were outside. She hoped so, since there hadn't been any arguments between them. But, as far as she knew, there hadn't been any words spoken, either.

In fact, the tension between them was so strong it filled the room, making everyone on edge. And to be honest, she was glad to see them go their separate ways.

As the vehicles began starting up outside, the guys leaving the girls to chat among themselves, Jenna said, "There's one thing that can be said. It's going to be interesting."

"What is?" Tammy asked.

"Getting to know each other, becoming the family we always should have been."

"Don't forget," Tammy added, "there might be one more of us."

"I'll never be able to forget that." Jenna sighed. "I can't help thinking that, if there is a love child, that he or she won't surface. If that happens, things are bound to blow sky-high."

"For what it's worth," Tammy said, "I already mentioned the receipt for the pregnancy test to my dad. And he asked me not to say anything. He said that he'd really like to honor Tex's wishes, but that news of a possible pregnancy would only throw salt on old wounds."

"To say the least," Jenna said.

Still, Tammy couldn't quench the nagging curiosity. "We could hire a P.I. to find out if there ever was a baby."

"I don't think it's up to the three of us to get that involved," Jenna said.

"Neither do I," Donna said. "Not that I wouldn't want to meet him or her. But it isn't any of our business."

"I'm not so sure about that. What do you say we have a vote."

"We kind of did that," Jenna said. "One maybe and two probably nots."

"Why don't we ask Aidan and Nathan when they return? In the meantime, the three of us could think about the positive and negative ramifications."

"We'd definitely need to think about it," Donna added, as she got up and headed for the kitchen. "If you'll excuse me, I'm going to fix a cup of tea."

At the sound of another vehicle engine, Tammy glanced out the window and spotted Mike driving up. He'd told her he'd stop by to see her after the reading of the will, and she was so glad that he had.

Ever since they'd admitted their true feelings, her love for him—and clearly his for her—had grown by leaps and bounds.

"Love is in the air," Jenna said.

Tammy turned to her cousin and smiled. "And I owe it all to you."

"I really didn't do anything."

"Yes, you did. You were a friend when I needed one

most. And I want you to know that I'll be hoping and praying that you meet the perfect guy soon, one who fits all the criteria on that list you made."

"My list." Jenna smiled. "I'll have to show it to you someday."

Tammy smiled. "You'll find the perfect guy."

"I know. And when I do, I hope I'm as lucky in love as you are."

Tammy looked out onto the porch, just as Mike approached. "It's more than luck. I've been truly blessed."

Then she walked outside and greeted Mike with a warm embrace and a kiss.

"Is it over?" he asked.

"Yes, and it went just as expected."

"Good. Do you feel like taking a walk?"

With him? She'd be up for anything, anytime. "Sure."

Mike took her by the hand, and she suspected he was leading her to the cabin.

"I just got off the phone with my mom," he said. "I told her about you and my decision to stay in Buckshot Hills. And she's going to book a flight so she can come out and visit. If she likes it, she might even consider moving here. The cost of living is so much cheaper here. So she'd be able to retire whenever she's ready."

Using her free hand, Tammy tucked a strand of hair behind her ear. "I hope she likes me."

Mike gave her hand a warm, gentle squeeze. "She's going to love you, just like I do."

And with that, he turned to Tammy and slowed to a stop. "I was going to take you back to the cabin and kiss you senseless. But I think I'll do that here."

"I'd like that," she said. "I'd like that a lot."

As Mike took her in his arms and placed his lips on hers, Tammy's heart darn near soared out of her chest.

Talk about dreams coming true...

Hers certainly had.

* * * * *

Will Jenna Byrd meet her match? Find out in
THE TEXAN'S FUTURE BRIDE
by Sheri Whitefeather,
the next installment in BYRDS OF A FEATHER!
On sale April 2013,
wherever Harlequin books are sold.

COMING NEXT MONTH
from Harlequin® Special Edition®
AVAILABLE MARCH 19, 2013

#2251 HER HIGHNESS AND THE BODYGUARD
The Bravo Royales
Christine Rimmer
Princess Rhiannon Bravo-Calabretti has loved only one man in her life—orphan turned soldier Captain Marcus Desmarais—but he walked away knowing that she deserved more than a commoner. Years later, fate stranded them together overnight in a freak spring blizzard...and gave them an unexpected gift!

#2252 TEN YEARS LATER...
Matchmaking Mamas
Marie Ferrarella
Living in Tokyo, teaching English, Sebastian Hunter flees home to his suddenly sick mother's side just in time to attend his high school reunion. Brianna MacKenzie, his first love, looks even better than she had a decade ago...but can he win her over for the second and final time?

#2253 MARRY ME, MENDOZA
The Fortunes of Texas: Southern Invasion
Judy Duarte
Because of a stipulation in her employment contract, Nicole Castleton needs to marry before she can become the CEO of Castleton Boots. Her plan to reunite with ex-high school sweetheart Miguel Mendoza was strictly business—until their hearts got in the way!

#2254 A BABY IN THE BARGAIN
The Camdens of Colorado
Victoria Pade
After what her great-grandfather did to his family, bitter Gideon Thatcher refuses to hear a word of January Camden's apology...or get close to the beautiful brunette. Plus, she's desperate to have a baby, and Gideon does *not* see children in his future. But after spending time together, they may find they share more than just common ground....

#2255 THE DOCTOR AND MR. RIGHT
Rx for Love
Cindy Kirk
Dr. Michelle Kerns has a "no kids" rule when it comes to dating men...until she meets her hunky neighbor who has a child—a thirteen-year-old girl to be exact! Her mind says no, but maybe this one rule *is* meant to be broken!

#2256 THE TEXAN'S FUTURE BRIDE
Byrds of a Feather
Sheri WhiteFeather
Suffering from amnesia, J.D. wandered aimlessly through Buckshot Hills until Jenna Byrd offered the injured cowboy a place to stay. Slowly memories flood back to him, but what he remembers makes him want to run away from love—*fast*. Yet why can't he keep himself out of beautiful Jenna's embrace?

You can find more information on upcoming Harlequin® titles,
free excerpts and more at www.HarlequinInsideRomance.com.

HSECNM0313

REQUEST YOUR FREE BOOKS!

2 FREE NOVELS PLUS 2 FREE GIFTS!

◈ HARLEQUIN®

SPECIAL EDITION

Life, Love & Family

YES! Please send me 2 FREE Harlequin® Special Edition novels and my 2 FREE gifts (gifts are worth about $10). After receiving them, if I don't wish to receive any more books, I can return the shipping statement marked "cancel." If I don't cancel, I will receive 6 brand-new novels every month and be billed just $4.49 per book in the U.S. or $5.24 per book in Canada. That's a savings of at least 14% off the cover price! It's quite a bargain! Shipping and handling is just 50¢ per book in the U.S. and 75¢ per book in Canada.* I understand that accepting the 2 free books and gifts places me under no obligation to buy anything. I can always return a shipment and cancel at any time. Even if I never buy another book, the two free books and gifts are mine to keep forever.

235/335 HDN FVTV

Name	(PLEASE PRINT)	
Address		Apt. #
City	State/Prov.	Zip/Postal Code

Signature (if under 18, a parent or guardian must sign)

Mail to the Harlequin® Reader Service:
IN U.S.A.: P.O. Box 1867, Buffalo, NY 14240-1867
IN CANADA: P.O. Box 609, Fort Erie, Ontario L2A 5X3

Want to try two free books from another line?
Call 1-800-873-8635 or visit www.ReaderService.com.

* Terms and prices subject to change without notice. Prices do not include applicable taxes. Sales tax applicable in N.Y. Canadian residents will be charged applicable taxes. Offer not valid in Quebec. This offer is limited to one order per household. Not valid for current subscribers to Harlequin Special Edition books. All orders subject to credit approval. Credit or debit balances in a customer's account(s) may be offset by any other outstanding balance owed by or to the customer. Please allow 4 to 6 weeks for delivery. Offer available while quantities last.

Your Privacy—The Harlequin® Reader Service is committed to protecting your privacy. Our Privacy Policy is available online at www.ReaderService.com or upon request from the Harlequin Reader Service.

We make a portion of our mailing list available to reputable third parties that offer products we believe may interest you. If you prefer that we not exchange your name with third parties, or if you wish to clarify or modify your communication preferences, please visit us at www.ReaderService.com/consumerschoice or write to us at Harlequin Reader Service Preference Service, P.O. Box 9062, Buffalo, NY 14269. Include your complete name and address.

HSE13

***

How could this have happened?

Rhiannon Bravo-Calabretti, Princess of Montedoro, could not believe it. Honestly. What were the odds?

One in ten, maybe? One in twenty? She supposed that it could have been just the luck of the draw. After all, her country was a small one and there were only so many rigorously trained bodyguards to be assigned to the members of the princely family.

However, when you added in the fact that Marcus Desmarais wanted nothing to do with her ever again, reasonable odds became pretty much no-way-no-how. Because he would have said no.

So why hadn't he?

A moment later she realized she knew why: because if he refused the assignment, his superiors might ask questions. Suspicion and curiosity could be roused, and he wouldn't have wanted that.

Stop.

Enough. Done. She was simply not going to think about it—about *him*—anymore.

She needed to focus on the spare beauty of this beautiful wedding in the small town of Elk Creek, Montana. Her sister was getting married. Everyone was seated in the little church.

Still, *he* would be standing. In back somewhere by the doors, silent and unobtrusive. Just like the other security people. Her shoulders ached from the tension, from the certainty he was watching her, those eerily level, oh-so-serious, almost-green eyes staring twin holes in the back of her head.

It doesn't matter. Forget about it, about him.

It didn't matter why he'd been assigned to her. He was there to protect her, period. And it was for only this one day and the evening. Tomorrow she would fly home again. And be free of him. Forever.

She could bear anything for a single day. It had been a shock, that was all. And now she was past it.

She would simply ignore him. How hard could that be?

***

Don't miss HER HIGHNESS AND THE BODYGUARD, coming in April 2013 in Harlequin® Special Edition®.

And look for Alice's story, HOW TO MARRY A PRINCESS, only from Harlequin® Special Edition®, in November 2013.

HARLEQUIN

SPECIAL EDITION

Life, Love and Family

Looking for your next
Fortunes of Texas: Southern Invasion fix?

Coming next month
MARRY ME, MENDOZA
by Judy Duarte

Because of a stipulation in her employment
contract, Nicole Castleton needs to marry before
she can become the CEO of Castleton Boots.
Her plan to reunite with former high school
sweetheart Miguel Mendoza was strictly
business—until their hearts got in the way!

*Available in April 2013 from Harlequin Special Edition
wherever books are sold.*